To: [redacted]

[redacted]

Sunstar
PUBLISHING LTD.

Readers interested in obtaining further information on the subject matter of this book are invited to correspond with
The Secretary, Sunstar Publishing, Ltd.
116 North Court Street, Fairfield, Iowa 52556

[redacted]

[redacted]

“THE FACE ON MARS”

By

Harold W.G. Allen

By the same author:

Ye Shall Know the Truth
The Edge of the Universe
Higher Perspective
The Eternal Universe
Cosmic Perspective

First Edition

Sunstar Publishing, Ltd.
116 North Court Street
Fairfield, Iowa 52556
U.S.A.

ISBN: 1-887472-27-4
Library of Congress Catalog Card Number: 97-065711

All persons portrayed in this novel are fictitious. Any resemblance between persons living or dead is coincidental.

Manufactured in the United States of America

"THE FACE ON MARS"

By Harold W.G. Allen

INTRODUCTION

Much of what passes today for science fiction should really be classified as fantasy fiction. In point of fact, genuine science is often conspicuous by its absence. Other than serving as mere "escapist" literature, little else is offered the reader. Of much greater worth is a book that is able to both entertain and impart knowledge. It is hereby contended that *The Face on Mars* poses a most unique blend of legitimate science, in conjunction with what is a truly believable fiction plot - one affording a generous and ample serving of such basic ingredients as adventure, suspense, mystery and drama.

With regard to the broad subject of science, it may be said that the past few centuries have given mankind an unprecedented insight into the structure of our physical universe, completely masking progress made in fields of philosophy and religion. But while science may have resolved many ancient mysteries, it has also managed to undermine a number of highly cherished beliefs. In effect, we are confronted with a situation in which sufficient information is now available to destroy old concepts - producing a vacuum in the minds of many inquisitive souls - without providing a much needed alternative!

As matters stand, there is presently little correlation of science with *Cause* or *Purpose*, in spite of strong indications that many of the clues and pieces to a giant cosmic jigsaw puzzle are readily available - clues whereby certain physical phenomena may now be seen to have roots buried deep in the realm of philosophy! Given proper incentive, there is every reason to suspect that many secrets of the universe will yield to the probing of an unbiased mind. Ultimately, an aroused curiosity - whether inspired by the most serious of philosophical works or science fiction - is bound to be reflected in terms of a richer perspective.

The strength of the scientific method lies in a willingness to subject theory to test. Frequently, circumstantial evidence must be resorted to in order to establish the validity of a premise. For this very reason there is always the risk of incurring error. (A graphic example of this would be widespread acceptance of the Big Bang theory of creation - a cosmology which is now revealed to be quite without foundation, being the product of incomplete laws of gravitation and an erroneous concept of radiation propagation.) Unlike the case with religious dogma, however, it is anticipated that a scientific falsehood will eventually be uncovered and the hypothesis discarded.

It is the expectation of the author that *The Face on Mars* will contribute a host of fresh ideas - from whence new truths may be found to replace inadequate concepts currently in vogue. There is also a fervent hope that it will stimulate a personal search for insight into the many wonders of the universe. If so, it shall have accomplished a primary function within the context of a most intriguing science fiction novel.

H.W.G.A.

THE UNIVERSE

Through distant ages man has gazed, with reverence, into the sky;
Foremost in his mind, that momentous question: Why?
How far are yonder points of light,
Shining like tiny beacons on the darkest night?
Whence came the stars, our heavenly host,
Their soft light shimmering like a phantom ghost?

Born of countless suns our Milky Way doth shine,
An enigma to ancient theories, which man must now refine.
Beyond the reaches of our Galaxy, in the enveloping depths of space,
Unnumbered starry systems participate in a truly cosmic race.
For the very universe is expanding, at a most prodigious rate;
Motivated, one would deduce, by Principle: a synonym for Fate.

H.W.G.A.

The Face On Mars

Chapter 1

2040 A.D.

The late afternoon sun glistened through the tall palm trees which surrounded the rented villa of Professor Matthew C. Duncan, a noted Canadian philosopher and linguist currently residing in the Florida community of Vero Beach. A sparkling blue swimming pool, its borders adorned with a profusion of semi-tropical vegetation, was inhabited by two children frolicking at the base of a small adjoining waterfall. Their parents, still clad in dry bathing attire, sat around a circular patio table at the opposite end of the pool, quite content to observe the playful antics.

"The twins certainly seem to be enjoying themselves," voiced the professor, glancing in their direction.

"They could almost pass for a pair of young porpoises," said Janet Thompson, a rather attractive brunette who appeared much too youthful to be the mother of 12-year-old twins.

Her husband, 35-year-old astronaut Adam J. Thompson, shifted slightly in his chair. "I'm sure going to miss the kids," he confessed.

"When do you have to leave?" asked his host.

"I report to Cape Canaveral for a final briefing session on Monday. Unless there is a change of plans, my shuttle is due to lift off for Space Station Prometheus next Friday. Needless to say, after months of practice in training modules we are quite anxious to get underway."

Further elaboration was interrupted by the arrival of a truly curvaceous blonde garnishing a bright red bikini and bearing tray of chilled orange juice. She also had with her a copy of the late edition of the *Vero Beach Chronicle*. "I do believe you will find this article to be of interest," she said, pointing to a headline which read: "Face on Mars to be Investigated."

"Thank you, Erica," said the professor. "It's about time Mission Control decided to take a close look at this peculiar feature, if only to resolve a lengthy controversy one way or the other."

First photographed by a Viking orbiter, in the 1970s, a rock structure on the Martian surface was discovered which looked remarkably like a human face. Some 1.5 kilometers in length, this intriguing cliff formation stood isolated from other mountains and hills. It did, in fact, appear to be the handiwork of a master race of humanoid sculptors instead of a fluke of nature. In spite of a series of later photos, it still invited a great deal of speculation. It would take a manned expedition to positively resolve the issue.

"What are your views, Matt?" asked his astronaut friend.

"I suppose the astronomers will ultimately be proven correct. The present consensus of opinion is that this unusual image is due to a combination of chance meteorite strikes and lighting effects. However, until such is proven to be the case I feel that it is in the best interest of science to visit this controversial object. If I have learned anything in my 33 years, it is that the universe is full of surprises," Professor Duncan answered.

"How far is this unique rock formation from your intended landing site?" Erica wanted to know.

Depositing his empty glass on the table, the bronzed 6'-2" tall astronaut pondered the question a moment before answering: "About 200 kilometers, I should venture to say. Our pressurized tractor vehicle was recently modified with the addition of extra storage batteries and solar cells."

"I'm beginning to wish that I had considered a career as a geologist, instead of earning a doctorate in philosophy and linguistics," lamented the professor. "I fear that my talents are not conducive to becoming a Martian explorer. By the way, Adam, what do you think chances are of finding water on Mars - that is, other than at the inhospitable polar ice caps, which can be much colder than the most severe Antarctic winter?"

"There is high expectation of uncovering sizable deposits in the form of permafrost, especially in regions which appear to be ancient river channels. The real issue is how deep it may lie beneath the surface. Although it is unlikely to happen in our lifetime, I can visualize a future Martian colony that will be self-sufficient with regard to both water and air."

It was Erica Williams, a fledgling 27-year-old astronaut (currently unassigned), who chose to elaborate: "Once water becomes available, oxygen can be separated from hydrogen by passing an electric current through it. As a further step the hydrogen in water, combined with carbon extracted from a Martian atmosphere rich in carbon dioxide, will produce methane fuel. In conjunction with oxygen, this mixture makes a rather good rocket propellant. Thus it will be seen that the eventual colonization of Mars is much more than science fiction."

"Indeed," continued the senior astronaut, "our probes of the Martian soil have already shown it to be an abundant source of many elements which could be mined to produce such items as cement, glass, plastics - to say nothing of a variety of useful metals."

"In short, it is merely a matter of time until the human race reaches out to populate other sections of our Solar System," Adam commented. "The capability and ingredients are all there."

"It is now the year 2040 A.D., barely more than seventy years since man first set foot on the Moon, less than a decade since completion of Earth orbiting Space Station Prometheus, and only a few years since the establishment of a lunar base," stated the professor. "At this rate I should think that a Martian colony is not out of the question by the end of the 21st century."

"Politicians have always challenged the wisdom of spending large sums of money for the exploration of space," said Erica. "What few seem to realize is a need for humanity to diversify in order to assure survival against some unforeseen calamity - whether it be the folly of nuclear/biological warfare, or a fluke collision with a massive asteroid body. There is also a great unifying force behind the necessity of many nations to cooperate in a joint venture - especially one featuring a harsh environment where disharmony could prove disastrous."

"I swear that if our glorious leaders - both political and religious - were exiled to Mars (or even the Moon) they would adopt a much broader perspective," Adam philosophized. "Having spent some time shuttling back and forth to international Lunar Colony, I can honestly testify as to the truly vast and wondrous nature of our universe. Petty squabbling and bickering over religious issues quickly invites revulsion. Nor does it seem to make any sense to strive for personal gain and material wealth, as safety of the community and harmony among one's colleagues assumes far greater importance."

"Clearly, what is urgently required is a World Government here on Earth - one in which resources are shared in a more equitable manner," opined Professor Duncan. "The sham that has passed for a United Nations organization, for these many years, is a disgrace to society."

"Amen to that assessment!" exclaimed Janet, turning slightly to better observe the children performing back flips into the deep end of the pool.

In point of fact it was only too true that, since its very inception almost a century earlier, United Nations had done little to abolish tyranny and injustice. Tolerating a long succession of obnoxious dictators, and doing nothing to prevent a host of minor nations from acquiring nuclear weapons, the world was in constant threat of terrorist groups. Sabotaging an airliner was now minor league action. Since the turn of the century no less than four low-yield atomic bombs had been detonated in retaliation for previous atrocities. All of these nefarious acts were perpetrated in the name of religion, or with selfish motives as the root cause. To the leaders of many "have-not" nations, atomic weaponry was both a status symbol and a means of intimidation.

Upon the world economic front, very little had been achieved in solving problems regarding inequality of wealth. Rich nations were still rich and poor nations still poor. Moreover, even the more prosperous countries continued to be plagued with substantial numbers of unemployed citizens, many of whom lived in poverty and resorted to crime. A succession of worthless election candidates always seemed to prevail, thereby upholding the credibility of critics in their belief that democracy was largely an illusion. Inasmuch as it cost a fortune to buy election publicity, ever since the advent of mass-media (radio, TV, newspaper chains, etc.) only the very rich (or their puppets) were likely to succeed. In order for the democratic process to work effectively, reasonable equality of wealth was clearly essential. Earth still awaited this heavenly day.

There was, however, a powerful contributing factor as to why many poor countries were destined to remain submerged in poverty. It concerned a manifest failure to curb a runaway birth rate. While inhabitants of the more progressive and enlightened nations generally practiced some form of birth control, large segments of the poorer countries were reluctant to adopt this common sense measure. Fueled, in most cases, by priestly pressure to subscribe to their convoluted views of quantity over quality, such gullible masses had pushed the world's population level to more than ten billion souls. This placed a severe strain upon the planet's food supply. Not only were all of the best fishing grounds badly depleted, but erosion now posed a major threat where forests had been stripped in a desperate attempt to grow ill-suited crops. Nature's constant menu of floods and drought was a perpetual cause of large-scale famine.

Yet another calamity had rather surreptitiously befallen Earth society over the course of the past century. While advances in medical science had done much to contain specific illnesses and prolong life, it was now becoming a stark reality that this very intervention was also undermining mankind's genetic base. It was a fact that a multitude of genetic defects were being passed on to future generations - defects that would not have been propagated in earlier times, simply because many carriers would have died before reaching puberty. (Examples of this would be such common genetically transmitted disorders as diabetes, cystic fibrosis, sickle cell anemia and hemophilia.) Without any screening of prospective parents, the birth of a healthy child was quickly becoming a game of Russian roulette. What many of the world's more advanced thinkers were now advocating was not a marriage license for young couples, but a birth license! At the rate by which the Earth's genetic pool was being degraded, it might not be long before almost every citizen would carry a serious genetic abnormality. In this respect, it was apparent that science and certain religious zealots were on an unexpected collision course.

It was Erica who raised the issue of science versus religion. "You know, I never cease to wonder at the intelligence level of some of these religious crackpots," she said, referring to another newspaper caption: "Evolution Repudiated by Noted Faith Healer."

"I'm afraid it's a case of logic being superseded by blind faith and fear of the unknown," voiced Professor Duncan.

"Indeed, some people will accept almost any philosophy to avoid thinking for themselves, especially if it offers what they want to believe," Erica added.

"We live in an age which is probably unique in the saga of the human race," continued the professor. "Science has managed to place many souls in somewhat of a vacuum. On the one hand, it has supplied sufficient evidence to negate the old biblical concept of special creation; while on the other, it has failed to provide a viable substitute."

"Adam tells me that you endorse the principle of reincarnation in several of your books. Do you think this philosophy affords a valid alternative?" asked Janet.

"Yes I do," replied the professor. "The very idea of having but one all-determining lifetime, in which to evolve spiritually, is really quite ludicrous. What, for instance, happens to the soul of an infant which dies prematurely? To say that it goes to a so-called heaven is totally absurd, if for no other reason than that it invites one to terminate its existence before it has had a chance to sin and jeopardize its destiny! Furthermore, at what stage of an individual's life are you going to impose such a mandatory time limit? At what year ... month ... week ... day ... hour ... minute ... second, etc.? Clearly, the entire scenario becomes ridiculous. Reincarnation, on the other hand, offers a very sensible solution to an otherwise intolerable situation. Most definitely, whatever status a soul possesses at the moment of biological death, so must it be perpetuated intact and be reborn into another physical body of similar caliber."

"But just how would you define a soul? By what criteria can we differentiate souls of unequal value?" Janet wanted to know.

The professor wasted little time in answering. "Philosophers and theologians have pondered this issue for ages," he replied. "In the last analysis, I believe that the simplest definition of a soul is probably the best - namely, that it consists of a degree or level of *unselfishness*. To the extent that one is willing to relinquish individualism in favor of One Harmonious Whole, so this feeling of Universal Love enables a soul to evolve spiritually."

"Then you accept the idea that there is a God or Principle governing the universe," Janet deduced.

"Indeed I do," Professor Duncan hastened to assure his guest. "But in no way do I subscribe to the naive biblical interpretation of a humanoid-type of God/Creator. A deity of this sort is purely the imagination of very primitive minds."

"I can readily see why, in order to inject the principle of justice into the universe, reincarnation could solve the mystery as to why a given soul should find itself inhabiting a specific body form: simply because, by reason of prior existence, it truly deserves to find itself situated where it does. But exactly how does evolution fit into the overall picture, professor?" asked Janet, much intrigued by the subject of reincarnation.

"In assessing the concept of evolution, we find that a rather striking parallel exists with respect to the traditional biblical view of but one all-determining lifetime. If man evolved from a microscopic origin, over immense periods of time, then where are we to draw a line as to when emerging man is blessed with the capability of passing to a mythical heaven? At what minute ... hour ... day ... year ... millennium, etc., does man suddenly become eligible for such a reward? Without a doubt, we have exactly the same problem which surfaces when we talk in terms of one all-determining lifetime. It must surely be that the answer to the one problem is also the solution to the other."

Reflecting momentarily upon the professor's words, Janet then asked: "How would you solve the enigma of an evolutionary heritage and the requirement that spirit be reborn into a succession of higher life forms?"

"By far the most obvious feature, in the chain of observed biological entities, is that of an increase in numbers at the lower levels. As a matter of fact," continued the professor, "the numbers of the more elementary life forms so greatly outnumber those of higher levels that the premise of reincarnation - in terms of individualism - becomes completely absurd. Advancement may only be achieved at the expense of a reduction in the numbers of spiritual entities. In short, many spirits of a low order must somehow combine to produce fewer spirits of a higher order through a process of *Cosmic Fusion.* This most logical deduction leads one to infer that the universe may be likened unto a vast pyramid-type structure, very wide at the base (signifying many entities of low value) and tapering to a point or pinnacle at the top where all is made Perfect in One Harmonious Whole: God. It must surely follow that there can be no stopping in a spirit's evolutionary progress toward Perfection. *Invariably, fusion into the One Body of God is the ultimate destiny of all creation - including that of mankind!"*

Both Janet and her husband displayed evidence of surprise and wonder at the prospect of such a glorious destiny. However, Erica seemed quite familiar and at ease with this highly revolutionary philosophy. It was apparent that, during the twelve months in which she had known the professor, a great deal of discussion had occurred between them. Unlike so many transitory relationships these days, there was more than a hint that physical attraction was not the sole ingredient, and that a definite spiritual bond already linked the couple.

Further indication of this union arose when Erica exclaimed: "Doesn't Matt's philosophy sound promising? For years I had been drifting in a sea of doubt and contradiction, fostered by parental beliefs in a literal interpretation of the Bible. Now I can see that the revelations of science and logic are infinitely superior to priestly tradition."

"Just what do you make of the various biblical stories?" Janet asked the professor. "Do you consider them to be worthless?"

"Not at all," he replied. "Many of the narratives convey a very instructive moral. Unfortunately, an endless procession of false prophets have turned this interesting body of literature into a nightmare of convoluted views and unfounded claims. In particular, they have completely glossed over a most unique form of symbolism - used throughout both the Old and New Testament - in order to express a specific principle. Although other symbols are used (such as *wine* or a *mountain* to signify inspiration, and a *stone* to depict the appearance of truth), by far the most used and most conspicuous symbols involve certain favored numbers. Hence, *one* is often used to impart the idea of but one God ruling the universe. The numeral *three* was adopted to portray insight into the truth. *Four* conveys a sense of seeking truth; while the *seven* represents completion or degree of perfection. The number *ten* was used to express the intentions or actions of man in his quest for truth. Finally, *twelve* was used to signify the universal extent and availability of divine principles. Also, it should be stated that there are times when *six* is used as a symbol of evil."

"Then you would conclude that much of the biblical literature was written for the purpose of conveying a moral or principle, and that historical fact was of quite secondary importance?" queried Janet.

"Precisely! The ancient scriptural writer's prime concern was with the spiritual aspect of matters. To them, mere physical and transitory events were inconsequential," answered the professor. "While they would use actual historical occurrences, if it suited their purpose, they were not beyond a measure of exaggeration or embellishment if they thought it would be accepted. In most cases their stories were written long after the events were supposed to have happened, thereby assuring that no witness could ever refute them."

"This concept of biblical symbolism promises to explain many mysteries," said Janet. "I had often wondered why such writings as Revelation, for example, were so permeated with repetitive numerals."

"I should point out that these so-called sacred numbers are sometimes used in a negative sense," cautioned the professor. "In other words, they can be used to express exactly the opposite meaning. Thus Peter's three denials of Jesus, along with three temptations by the devil (a symbol of ignorance), are intended to illustrate lack of insight into the truth. A prime example of a number used in the normal positive sense would be the genealogy purporting to trace Jesus' ancestry back to the mythical Adam. It should come as no great surprise to find that Jesus is listed as the 77th son! In the other genealogy attempt, which traces back to Abraham, it is noted that there are three groups of fourteen (ten plus four) names. Incidentally, I should also mention that there are occasions when certain numbers are used in a multiplied sense, the most significant of which is the four and the ten (making forty) - conveying a sense of seeking the truth with the intention of putting knowledge to use. Accordingly, we have such instances as Jesus fasting forty days in the wilderness, along with the forty days of rain in the allegorical Noah story."

"What I still find puzzling is the contradictory portrayal of Jesus as both God and human being," said Janet.

Instinctively, the professor knew that the passages to which she referred could be summed up in two statements: "my Father is greater than I" (John 14:28); "I and my Father are one" (John 10:30). As an unbiased student of biblical literature he had long since deduced that

"Christ" is a *hypothetical* title or goal. In essence, it symbolizes the principle of one striving toward the ultimate goal of Perfection - in which sense it might well be said that "I am the way, the truth, and the life: no man cometh unto the Father, but by me" (John 14:6). He hastened to convey this interpretation to his charming and inquisitive guest.

"I must agree with the logic behind your assessment," conceded Janet. "But why was this symbolic portrayal lost and distorted by subsequent generations?"

"To understand how this regrettable state of affairs came to be we must consider the issue of Christian origins in the light of ancient Jewish beliefs of a Messiah - a deliverer who would come and establish a new world order," began the professor. "Since it is often advantageous to tell people what they want to hear, there was always the temptation to embellish an account written after the fact. As was eventually established, through analysis of the Dead Sea Scrolls, the apostle Paul (who never met Jesus) was the chief proponent of a Jesus/God deity."

"I seem to recall reading something about the Dead Sea Scrolls controversy," voiced Janet. "Wasn't there a claim that orthodox religious leaders had been guilty of suppressing information?"

"Indeed they did!" exclaimed Professor Duncan. "Discovered over a period of years during the 20th century, in numerous caves scattered around the Dead Sea, publication of certain of these ancient scrolls was needlessly delayed for decades by factions fearful of their contents. What they finally revealed was that the original followers of Jesus did not entertain any notion at all of his divinity! In fact, it was for this very claim that James (the brother of Jesus) was so critical of Paul, and which ultimately resulted in his persecution."

"Then how did the concept of God/Jesus ever gain such a strong foothold?" Janet wanted to know.

"A greater mystery would be why this gross misconception has persisted to this very day," opined the professor. "However, to answer your question, it is necessary to consider the influence of another competing religion which flourished in Rome during the days of the early Christians. Known to scholars as Mithraism, it was an ancient Persian religion which had been adopted by many of the Roman military before the time of Jesus. Embracing the idea of a Redeemer or Mediator between God and mankind (which is quite against the principle of free will!), it prevailed until the 4th century A.D., when it finally succumbed to the new religion that we now call Christianity. Actually, it would be more accurate to describe it as a merger, since many of the chief features of this older cult were absorbed into the structure of its successor - including the practice of observing Christmas upon the birthday of Mithras himself! Other ideas borrowed from Mithraism include changing the Jewish Sabbath to Sunday (the holy day of Mithras), along with notions of a mystical salvation from a eucharistical Last Supper. It was just a short step to turn a Redeemer/Mediator into a Jesus/Christ deity."

"I had always wondered why Christmas is celebrated on December 25th, when there is not the slightest hint of Jesus' birthday in the biblical record," Janet confessed.

Professor Duncan continued: "Until this fateful merger with Mithraism, there is every reason to assume that many of the early followers of Jesus accepted the principle of reincarnation, since it was not an unpopular philosophy during his lifetime and at no time did he see fit to repudiate it! On the contrary, the very statement that 'In my Father's house are many mansions' (John 14:2) does seem to suggest belief in reincarnation philosophy. In any event, history reveals that among the more prominent of the early Christians who accepted the concept of reincarnation were Origen, St. Augustine, and St. Francis of Assisi."

It was Erica who now entered into the dialogue. "Why has this theological deceit been allowed to persist?" she asked.

"I'm afraid that tradition often dies hard," the professor replied. "Nevertheless, it is apparent that substantial numbers of churchgoers are seriously questioning many archaic dogmas - including unfounded objection to birth control, medical abortion, and the wholly unethical concept of a Redeemer. This has resulted in much bickering, and subsequent dissolution into many Christian and Moslem sects differing widely in both creed and motivation. Some continue to be a passive force within society, content to let others forge their own destiny, while affording consolation to those fearful of the unknown. Unfortunately, a number of highly militant religious factions have arisen of late, some of whom pose a definite threat to the advancement of the human race."

Silent for some time, astronaut Adam Thompson spoke. "Are you referring to the recent rash of shootings and bombings involving medical and scientific establishments?" he inquired.

"Yes I am," replied the professor. "I am alarmed at the sharp escalation of these terrorist attacks. First it was just abortion clinics, doctors and staff. Then their targets were expanded to include owners, editors and publishing houses printing opposing points of view. Now they have resorted to sabotaging a number of genetic laboratories, along with several radio telescopes engaged in a search for extraterrestrial life forms. One wonders if this insanity will ever end."

"I swear there are times when I don't know who constitutes the greater threat to society: religious zealots or racially motivated terrorists," lamented Erica.

"Perhaps we should all escape to Mars," proposed Adam.

"Hopefully, the dangers of space will prove to be the lesser of evils," said his wife, again turning to look at the children who seemed quite at home in their host's pool.

"Why don't we join them before eating?" suggested Professor Duncan. "I believe Erica has programed dinner for seven o'clock."

"An excellent idea," agreed the Mars-bound astronaut, knowing that it might well be his last opportunity to swim for a very long time.

Somewhat later, refreshed and with contented stomachs, they watched as the first stars of evening appeared. Conversation was soon diverted to talk of the heavens, being given further impetus when the planet Mars became clearly discernible. For many years a keen amateur astronomer, Professor Duncan had promised to give the children a crash course in essentials of the starry universe. To this end he was busily engaged in setting up his treasured 12-inch reflecting telescope. With images enhanced by CCD electronics, and connected to a computer and a 40-inch TV screen, one had only to push a few buttons in the comfort of one's living room in order to view many faint cosmic wonders.

The two 12-year-old Thompson twins, Robert and Susan, seemed delighted to learn that they would be able to view many distant celestial objects on a TV screen. Amateur astronomy had come a long way during the past few decades. No longer was it necessary to squint through a tiny eyepiece attached to a telescope. Nor did one have to spend an inordinate amount of time scanning the sky in an attempt to locate some wayward body or star system. By simply punching the coordinates into a computer it was possible for even a novice to be rewarded with success.

At last the professor announced that all was ready. "What would you like to view first?" he asked of his audience.

It was a question that need not have been raised. The initial choice, of course, was the planet Mars.

"Will we be able to see the mysterious Martian face?" Susan wanted to know, having been intrigued by the photograph which had accompanied the newspaper report inspiring earlier conversation.

"I'm afraid not," replied the professor, pointing out that it was far too small to be seen with his modest instrument. "To view it with my little telescope it would be necessary to put it into orbit around the planet," he added.

Activation of a series of buttons promptly revealed a small reddish-brown sphere. As they watched, the white north polar ice cap and a number of dark surface markings soon became visible. Increased magnification served to produce a larger image, but it failed to give the clarity obtained in photos taken by orbital probes. In this sense, the TV image before them was somewhat of a disappointment to the children, especially since their father had exposed them to numerous high resolution close-up pictures.

"In another three months or so the separation between our two worlds will be only about one-half of the present distance," the professor informed the children. "Now close to 100 million miles away in its journey around the Sun, this distance is being reduced steadily as our faster moving Earth is in the process of gradually overtaking Mars."

Attention soon shifted to other planets of the Solar System that were conveniently situated in the night sky. Jupiter, with its four largest moons (Io, Europa, Ganymede and Callisto) clearly visible, was the second object to be viewed. Readily apparent to the observers were a number of colorful equatorial cloud bands, displaying subtle shades of orange, brown, gray, yellow, cream and light blue. Some 318 times more massive than Earth, the planet spun rapidly about its axis in just a trifle more than 9 hours and 50 minutes, which explained the oblate appearance of this gas giant. Orbiting the Sun at a distance equal to roughly five times that of Earth, it required twelve of our years to make one full circuit.

The next planet to be observed was Saturn, some 95 times the mass of Earth and almost twice the distance of Jupiter from the Sun. With its year equal to nearly 30 Earth years, it likewise exhibited equatorial bands and displayed an oblate silhouette due to a rotation period of little more than 10.5 hours. By far its most distinguishing feature was its unique series of rings, which served to double the planet's apparent size when viewed in open pattern. Composed of myriads of tiny bodies - largely chunks of ice or ice-coated rock - Saturn seemed to exude a certain charm that set it apart from the other planets. Titan, largest of its family of moons, was visible as a faint 8th magnitude companion. Slightly bigger than Mercury, it possessed a relatively dense atmosphere of liquid nitrogen (plus lesser amounts of liquid methane and other compounds) which made it opaque to telescopic view.

Moving beyond the confines of the Solar System, it was decided to view regions of recent star formation. The Orion Nebula was the first to receive attention. Near the center of the nebula shone four bright stars clustered close together to form the corners of a square presented to us at an angle. Known as the Trapezium stars, they are relatively young - possibly, of the order of 100,000 years. The dark outline of the rather striking Horsehead Nebula was also viewed. An opaque concentration of dust (in the shape of a horse's head), it was contrasted against a region glowing red with the light of hydrogen gas excited by the presence of luminous stars. It was truly an impressive sight.

The Pleiades cluster, believed to be almost 100 million years old, was the next object to be projected on the screen. Strongly resembling a condensed and truncated version of the Big Dipper, this star cluster is located in the constellation of Taurus at a distance of some 400 light-years. (A light-year may be defined as the distance that a ray of light is able to travel in one year, at a speed of approximately

186,000 miles per second - roughly, equal to circling the Earth more than 7.5 times every second.) The blue-white nebulosity enveloping the star Pleione, one of the brighter cluster members, was a classic feature of a massive and youthful star. With an equatorial velocity of close to 190 miles per second, this star is spinning so fast as to literally spew rings of hydrogen gas into space.

"Why is this star rotating so fast?" Robert asked, showing more than casual interest.

"An excellent question," replied his astronomer host. "Rapid rotation is actually the normal state of affairs when a new star forms out of a contracting gas cloud. Indeed, it is the mechanism by which solar systems are born, as a family of planets is almost certain to condense out of these expelled rings of gas and dust. The very fact that all planets of our Solar System revolve in the same direction, and on virtually the same plane as the Sun's equator, must be considered strong evidence of just such an event. Largely through a process of magnetic interaction, a young star's rapid rotation is greatly reduced at the expense of pushing these rings of planetary material away from the center of mass - in full conformity to a law of physics known as conservation of angular momentum."

"Does this mean that all stars have planets?" Robert wanted to know.

"It indicates that large numbers of planetary systems must have formed, of which a reasonable proportion may be expected to resemble our own Solar System," answered the professor. "If only one percent of these were to prove fruitful, it would imply that billions of planetary systems must populate our Milky Way galaxy. It is not unreasonable to assume that at least tens of millions of planets, similar in all essential respects to Earth, are destined to arise."

"Will we ever get to talk to them?" asked Susan, sharing her brother's interest in celestial matters.

"I would think the chances of contacting another civilization are rather good," answered the professor. "However, the average distance between stars is so great that it could take centuries just to send a message and receive a reply. On the other hand, the reward for establishing contact is bound to be enormous."

"Why is that?" Robert inquired.

Professor Duncan undertook to explain: "It is simply because we have only reached the technological stage where we are able to communicate via the radio telescope. By the laws of probability, any responding civilization is most likely to have acquired this capability many thousands (or millions) of years earlier. Hence, whoever we finally manage to contact will almost certainly be far more advanced than ourselves. The mind boggles at the thought of what they could teach us."

"How do we know they won't want to invade us?" asked Susan, obviously much influenced by exposure to TV cartoons.

"It is almost inconceivable that a society capable of space travel could have failed to evolve spiritually," philosophized the professor. "Unless a reasonable balance is maintained between technological prowess and moral integrity, it is highly probable that a civilization would end up destroying itself long before the advent of interstellar travel. Even now, it is anything but a certainty that the human race is able to live indefinitely with the threat of the H-bomb."

"So you see, if any spacefaring society is a menace to its galactic neighbors, it is likely to be ourselves who turn out to be the villain," Erica explained.

With the children thus assured of the desirability and safety of establishing extraterrestrial contact, attention shifted to a remarkable celestial object known as the Crab Nebula. Located in the constellation of Taurus, about 4,000 light-years away, this blue-green nebula is the remnant of a supernova explosion - the light of which only reached us in the year 1054 A.D., roughly 4,000 years after the event occurred. Near the center of this expanding cloud of gas and dust lay a neutron star, its rapid rotation causing it to pulsate some 30 times each second to an observer situated on Earth.

Defining such a flashing object as a pulsar promptly elicited two questions from Robert. "What produces a pulsar/neutron star? Why did this star explode as a supernova?" he asked.

Encouraged by Robert's interest, Professor Duncan proceeded to offer a brief synopsis of stellar evolution:

"The final size of a newly condensed star is the outcome of two opposing forces. On the one hand, we have the familiar force of gravitation, which acts to draw all matter toward a central point. In contrast, we have the repulsive force of heat, which tends to disperse matter into space. Stability is achieved when the internal temperature of a youthful condensing star becomes sufficient to support the weight of outlying regions, halting all contraction and resulting in a main-sequence star like our Sun. The temperature of a newly formed star is very much determined by its mass, in the sense that the heavier the star the higher the temperature. Initially, this heat is derived through compression induced by gravity, but when rising core temperature reaches a critical value it permits nuclear reactions to occur - a process whereby hydrogen is fused into helium with the release of a steady and substantial flow of energy.

"The evolution of a star is determined primarily by its mass. However, instead of more hydrogen enabling it to burn longer, quite the reverse is seen to be the case. This is because higher mass produces a hotter core temperature which, in turn, causes a rapid - and totally disproportionate - increase in the rate of nuclear reactions. Thus a main-sequence star which is only twice as massive as our Sun may radiate ten times as much energy. As a result, stars of high mass must consume their fuel in just a small fraction of the time required by much slower burning lightweights. A massive star may well consume its resources in mere millions of years; while one of little mass is capable of burning for tens of billions of years. Our Sun is believed to be about five billion years old and is likely able to continue without any significant change for a few billion more. But once change does occur some very profound events will transpire in a relatively short time.

"As a star consumes its hydrogen fuel a dense central core of helium accumulates and continues to grow, along with higher and higher temperatures induced by gravitational contraction of a region now deficient in nuclear energy production. In turn, core temperature escalation causes hydrogen burning reactions to spread over a greater volume of a star's interior - literally forcing the outer layers to expand apart. Eventually, such a star might well swell to more than a hundred times its original size: an inflated red giant star.

"In terms of a star's lifetime, this bloated state does not last very long before exhaustion of fuel leads to an inevitable collapse. A star at this stage of its life is capable of becoming a pulsating object, as heat generated from contraction results in temporary expansion until gravity once more prevails. Pulsating stars have played a major role in extending the galactic distance scale, since it was discovered that their rhythmic pattern is linked to intrinsic luminosity - in the sense that stars with long pulsation periods are far more luminous than those exhibiting short periods. Inasmuch as one strain of pulsating star (Cepheid variable) is of very high luminosity, it has permitted astronomers to determine stellar distances considerably beyond the limitation of any trigonometry method.

"As such stars continue their gradual collapse, many are able to shed a portion of mass by periodically puffing out shells of material. For them contraction is permitted to continue far past their initial main-sequence dimensions until, finally, degenerate electron pressure becomes sufficient to support the weight of the star's outlying regions and a level of stability is attained: a white dwarf. A star of this nature may be visualized as one which has managed to compress roughly the mass of our Sun (about 330,000 Earths) into a sphere closely resembling the Earth in size.

"A rather violent fate awaits stars of excessive mass. With still higher internal temperatures the helium core begins to burn and create a succession of heavier elements which, in turn, are caused to burn in layers extending outward from the doomed star's center. Eventually, and subsequent to a large-scale production of iron, the stage becomes set for a mammoth fireworks display. For once a critical core temperature/density is reached, an abrupt breakdown of iron nuclei occurs, absorbing energy and causing an implosion of the core. Following a prompt rebound, a substantial portion of the star's mass is literally blasted into the depths of space: a supernova explosion. Thus does nature contrive to create and spread a mixture of heavier elements into uncondensed clouds of primordial hydrogen gas - clouds which are now able to give rise to new generations of stars enriched with the ingredients needed to form Earth-type planets. It is to supernovae explosions that we owe our very existence, as all the atoms of our bodies (other than hydrogen) were once ejected from massive stars which had neared the end of their evolutionary cycle.

"The eventual fate of a supernova core remnant hinges upon the factor of mass. If the mass involved is no more than a few solar masses, it is likely to end up as a rapidly rotating neutron star or pulsar, possibly no more than 20 kilometers across. As compact as such an object may be, it is far from the last word in cosmic density. With only a minor contraction beyond this state, it is theorized that gravitation will overcome the inherent repulsive fields of atomic nuclei - producing a total collapse into what is commonly referred to as a stellar black hole: a truly super cosmic particle with a mass in excess of several solar masses contracted into all but spatial oblivion!"

Concluding his dialogue on stellar evolution, Professor Duncan entered a new series of instructions into the computer controlling his telescope. This time he sought out the globular cluster M15, in the constellation of Pegasus. Almost 35,000 light-years away, and barely visible to the naked eye as a hazy patch of light, this seemingly unimpressive object was soon resolved into a magnificent spherical clumping of closely packed stars. Estimated to contain 100,000 suns, it was but one of the close to 200 globular clusters so believed to orbit the central bulge of our Milky Way galaxy. Deduced to be about 13 billion years old from a study of the way in which its stars have evolved off the main-sequence, it has long been acknowledged that these ancient clusters provide valuable clues concerning the formation of galactic systems.

The last object to be viewed for the evening was the beautiful spiral galaxy known as M31, in the constellation of Andromeda. Regarded as a near twin to our Milky Way, with a mass of hundreds of billions of stars, it lay a little over two million light-years distant. Under ideal viewing conditions this great star system is visible to the unaided eye as a slightly elongated and faint patch of light, almost rivaling the Moon in size. Projected upon the TV screen, its central regions displayed a yellowish glow due to the prevalence of older yellow and red stars. In contrast, the spiral arms shone with a bluish tinge by reason of a young population of massive stars. A number of globular clusters could be seen in close association. Also visible, in the form of twin satellite systems, were NGC 205 and M32. Together with our Milky Way and its two Magellanic Cloud satellites, a smaller spiral system known as M33 and about two dozen (mostly dwarf irregular) galaxies, such nearby systems comprise what has been termed the Local Group.

Sensing the children's disappointment upon terminating the viewing session, the professor hastened to placate them. "Perhaps we can continue our observations next weekend," he said. "Your mother has accepted our invitation to stay with us for a few days after your father leaves for Mars."

Rewarded by a chorus of vocal applause, it was not long before his guests made their departure and the professor was left alone with Erica.

"It must be a terrible feeling to know that it will be almost a year until your family could be united," she remarked.

"I just hope that nothing goes wrong," he said, fully aware of the many hazards that could plague man's first voyage to Mars.

Seated with Erica beside the pool, Professor Duncan soon found himself contemplating the circumstances of his chance meeting with Adam. It was on a tennis court at Toronto's York University, some ten years ago, that they had first met. Born and raised in a suburb of this sprawling city, Matt was taking a post-graduate course; while Adam was a visiting speaker describing America's space program. (He even remembered the tennis score: a close third set tie-breaker that had gone 7-5 in his favor.) Since then the two had become best of friends, both on and off the tennis court. It was Adam, in fact, who had introduced him to Erica almost a year ago.

Initially a registered nurse with a keen interest in space medicine, Erica had joined the astronaut training program and might soon be required to spend four months aboard Space Station Prometheus. He did not like the prospect of being separated from this 27-year-old beauty that he had come to love. At least they would be able to spend the next three weeks together. After that it would be back to work at his teaching position at a nearby university, now that his sabbatical (taken in order to complete a textbook) had almost expired.

"What are you thinking?" she asked, noting his pensive mood.

"I was wondering what fate has in store for us," he replied, aware that she had once voiced similar thoughts.

"Why don't we enjoy one day at a time?" she reasoned. "Very often quality of a relationship can make up for quantity."

He reached over and planted a gentle kiss on her lips. "Let's go for a quick swim before turning in," he suggested.

They both stood up and began to disrobe. With the subdued glow of an underwater light providing minimal illumination, they quickly removed the last vestige of clothing and plunged into the warm water. Swimming little more than a lap, their nude bodies came together and they could not resist a passionate embrace. As her twin peaks firmed immediately to his delicate touch, so his unsheathed maleness became similarly aroused. An urgent retreat to the bedroom was clearly indicated.

Exiting the pool they chanced to glance upward at the planet Mars, its amber color setting it apart from the other celestial bodies. They had no way of knowing just how much this distant world would shortly change both their lives and, indeed, the very course of Earth history.

Chapter 2

JOURNEY TO MARS

Although tentative plans to visit Mars had been drawn up soon after the turn of the 21st century, lack of funding had put the ambitious project on hold until the year 2030 A.D. At this time NASA entered into agreement with a consortium of nations to supply both components and astronauts. Chief among these contributors were Russia, China, Japan and Great Britain. Also involved, to a slightly lesser extent, were a host of European countries, Canada, Australia and Brazil. In many respects, it could be considered a global undertaking.

Unfortunately, the most fuel efficient return trip to Mars was far from the shortest, requiring more than 2.5 years. Very few scientists (and no astronauts) were in favor of such a lengthy mission. In terms of extra expendables (i.e., water, air, food), it would certainly be equivalent to a substantial amount of fuel. After giving the matter some thought it was finally decided to go with a plan which would require somewhat more fuel in order to reduce time by a significant factor. The itinerary called for an outbound voyage of three months and a return trip of six months. This schedule allowed for a maximum stay of one month, either on the Martian surface or in orbit.

The next decision involved selecting a propulsion system. While the concept of a nuclear-electric rocket engine was given due consideration, it was eventually discarded on the grounds that a reliable ion engine had yet to be perfected. (Delivering very modest but sustained thrust, it did afford a much higher ratio of thrust to weight.) This left a choice between solid fuel chemical rockets and liquid fuel propellants. Both had their advantages and disadvantages. The superiority of solid over liquid lay in the simplicity and ease of handling of the former. The great disadvantage was that it could not be turned off and would burn until fully exhausted. Thus it was evident that at least some liquid fueled engines had to be used, if for no other purpose than to perform mid-course corrections, orbital maneuvers and eventual Mars touchdown. A compromise between the two propulsion fuels was the final choice of the experts.

Design of the main spacecraft featured a total of no less than 96 solid fuel rockets, divided into two wing pods extending on opposite sides of a long cylindrical fuselage. Joined together by a latticework of connecting struts, small explosive charges would permit ejection of expended rockets in order to eliminate useless weight. At the far end of the Mars Voyager, as the historic craft was called, was a battery of four liquid fueled engines. Located at strategic positions were a number of tiny thrusters, which facilitated orientation of the big spaceship.

A sizable dish antenna protruded from the front end of the craft. Directed toward Earth, it would provide both radio and TV communication, even if it might take as long as five minutes for a signal to make the journey from the vicinity of the Red Planet. An even more conspicuous appendage to the body of the Mars Voyager was a unique rotating wheel crew compartment. Situated at the end of a short pedestal projecting from the top of the fuselage, and midway between the two opposing wing pods of solid fuel rockets, this hollow wheel structure permitted a measure of artificial gravity. Four connecting tubes attached the wheel to the central pedestal. The wheel itself was divided into four chambers with adjoining airtight doors.

A compact but efficient nuclear reactor was placed near the end of the highly elongated fuselage, where it would receive a maximum degree of shielding surrounded by clusters of spherical fuel tanks. It was engineered to supply the bulk of the craft's electrical needs. Tanks of water and oxygen were concentrated amidships; while the forward compartment housed communication and radar equipment. Adjoining this electronics module was a dual purpose lounge and dining room. A small kitchen, several storage cabinets and a lavatory were situated just aft of these foremost bulkheads. A second lavatory, along with an exercise room, was located within one of the four rotating wheel chambers.

The main control center was built into a metallic bubble atop the revolving wheel pedestal. When in use it was necessary for them to discontinue the artificial gravity, otherwise rotation would tend to make its inhabitants rather dizzy. Adorned with a generous complement of porthole windows, it afforded the crew an opportunity to view the heavens without recourse to externally mounted TV cameras. A modest but quite adequate 14-inch remotely controlled telescope provided the astronauts with their very own astronomical observatory.

Attached to the underside of the mother ship was a somewhat smaller combination landing craft and ascent vehicle. Similar in certain respects to the first lunar lander, the Explorer was much larger. The chief difference was a curved heat shield built into its lower end, through which protruded four shock absorbing legs that were also protected by the same ceramic temperature resistant material. Although relying heavily upon rocket engines to slow their descent, this aeroshell structure would allow the astronauts to make use of the thin Martian atmosphere as a braking medium. Yet another feature designed to utilize the presence of the Red Planet's atmospheric gasses was a sturdy drag-chute incorporated into the craft's upper ascent stage, where it would be deployed upon achieving a specific reduction of velocity.

Whereas the descent module contained two liquid fueled rocket motors, the smaller return vehicle had but one powerful central engine which fired directly through the open passageway connecting the two stages. A large hatch/landing ramp was situated at the bottom of this cylindrical tube, which gave access to the upper stage via an air lock. Needless to say, it would be left open at the moment of liftoff so as to vent the hot exhaust gasses of the ascent engine.

The interior of both stages was filled, for the most part, by huge fuel tanks. Much smaller containers held such consumables as water and oxygen. The lower descent module also contained two items vital to man's planned exploration of the Martian surface. A compact portable nuclear reactor was considered essential as a means of supplying the electrical energy required for a variety of functions - including the need for heat during the bitterly cold nights. The second item was a pressurized Rover tractor, designed to provide both transportation and protection from a harsh and practically airless environment.

The command center of the two stages was, of necessity, built into the top portion of the upper stage. Occupying approximately one-fourth of the module's total volume, this pressurized section constituted both living quarters and control station. A series of oval windows permitted a limited but adequate view. Adjacent to the drag-chute compartment was a folded radio/TV antenna system, which would be extended once the craft had landed. Groups of tiny nozzles, scattered around the aluminum alloy hull, facilitated all small-scale maneuvering and orientation of the Explorer.

Crucial to assembly of the Mars Voyager was Earth's orbiting Prometheus, which had been completed in 2033 A.D. Much larger than previous space stations, it looked like a giant four-spoke wheel (with a glistening metallic tire) rolling slowly across the heavens. Simulating gravity, by means of centrifugal force, it permitted man to more readily adapt to prolonged periods in space. Already, an array of large optical telescopes - located within the station's central hub - had rewarded mankind with a veritable wealth of knowledge, especially in wavelengths not conducive to observation through our planet's atmosphere. However, in terms of planetary exploration, its greatest contribution was to provide a base of operations for the dozens of workers who had toiled for several years assembling a multitude of spaceship components which had been ferried up from Earth. This labor was currently on the verge of justification, as the seven adventurous astronauts now aboard Prometheus were about to embark on man's greatest pioneering venture into space.

Selection of this historic crew had been anything but an easy task. Choosing an expedition leader was almost as difficult. By reason of his greater experience the veteran Russian astronaut, Boris Brodsky, was finally given command of the Mars Voyager. A skilled pilot and superb navigator, the 39-year-old favorite spoke fluent English, the official language for the mission. Like his American counterpart, Adam Thompson, this 6'-1" tall astronaut was leaving behind a wife, one son and one daughter.

A second Russian crew member was Georgi Maladev. Also an experienced pilot/navigator, the likeable 38-year-old blonde had been designated as one of the two members scheduled to remain in Mars orbit while his companions departed for the surface. Only moderately disappointed by this decision, he was thrilled just to be making the trip. Unlike his fellow countryman, Maladev had never married and was still a carefree 5'-9" bachelor.

The other astronaut chosen to remain aboard the mother ship was Kishi Yamoto, a 36-year-old Japanese electronics specialist. Among his achievements was an excursion to Earth's first lunar base, where he played a key role in setting up a number of highly sophisticated electronic devices. He was also well versed in the operation of small nuclear reactors, having originally studied to become a physicist. Shortest member of the expedition, at 5'-7", he had a wife and 10-year-old daughter.

China's contribution to the Mars mission was 35-year-old Chou Lin, a talented physicist who had participated in development of the portable nuclear reactor constructed for the Explorer landing craft. It was largely for this reason that he was selected to accompany the adventurers to the Martian surface. One additional factor leading to this decision could be traced to an earlier incident on Prometheus, when his expertise was called upon in order to avoid a potential problem with the station's reactor. Married, with one son, 5'-8" Lin was considered to be a valuable acquisition to the crew roster.

Fulfilling the role of physician to the expedition was one of England's most respected microbiologists, 38-year-old Dr. Jeffery Walker. Author of numerous papers on the very relevant subject of space medicine, he had long been an advocate of man's need to explore the planet Mars. The only member of the crew to sport a mustache, this 5'-11" tall scientist was quite popular with his colleagues. Recently widowed due to a tragic accident, he had been reluctant to leave his 14-year-old daughter. To the relief of Mission Control, she had finally managed to convince him that his destiny lay in space.

The remaining astronaut was 39-year-old geologist Martin A. Chadwick, a distinguished American whose book on lunar geology had received worldwide acclaim. His first-hand experience, obtained during the course of three visits to the Moon, easily outclassed all competitors. If any man could unravel the history of Martian topography it would be this slightly balding 5'-8" truly dedicated scientist. Chadwick was happily married with a 16-year-old son. By the time his father returned he would very likely be entering university.

Their last briefing concluded, the seven Mars-bound astronauts waved a dramatic farewell to a TV audience estimated to exceed one billion viewers. Proceeding through a docking air lock, it was not long before they left Prometheus and entered a waiting shuttle craft. Parked a scant 1,000 meters away was the Mars Voyager, its silver hull glistening in bright sunshine. In a matter of minutes the crew was transferred from the tiny ferry module to the giant spaceship. Picking up a small maintenance group that had finished conducting a series of final checks, the shuttle soon returned to its berth at the hub of the rotating space station. For better or for worse, the adventurers were now on their own.

The orbit of Prometheus had been purposely designed so as to facilitate the launch of a manned expedition to Mars. Not only would proper orientation simplify departure, but it would save a certain amount of precious fuel. Periodically, in their journey around Earth, they would be aimed in just the right direction. By igniting their rocket engines at this time their orbital motion (almost 17,600 mph) would be fully conserved. This optimum launch window was fast approaching.

"All set?" Brodsky asked, assured that all of his companions were securely strapped into their acceleration couches.

"Let's go!" exclaimed Yamoto, echoing the wishes of his fellow crew members.

Upon receiving the command, Thompson flipped the two switches which ignited the first pair of rockets, one on either side of the dual wing pods, so as to preserve maximum stability. Immediately, they could feel a return of the force of gravity, even if it was due to acceleration rather than the normal influence imposed by the presence of some massive body. A second pair was soon fired, pushing them deeper into their foam padded seats and sending a new surge of motion throughout the entire ship. A third and fourth pair were ignited at appropriate intervals, as their predecessors burned out and were promptly jettisoned. Eventually, the whole outer tier of solid fuel rockets were either burning or had been discarded. Surpassing escape velocity from Earth's gravitational pull (some 11.2 kilometers per second), the Mars Voyager hurtled outward in a curved trajectory that would take them ever further from the Sun. Still more rockets were fired in a very carefully arranged sequence. Man was now traveling away from his native planet with a velocity scarcely dreamed of a mere century ago.

A steady green light on a control panel revealed which rockets were in a state of ignition; while a flashing red light disclosed the presence of those members that had been exhausted. The flip of a specific switch would detonate small explosive charges in the tubular framework which secured the burned out rockets. One by one the empty casings were discarded into the depths of space. By the time the astronauts returned to Earth they would be manning a much slimmer spaceship - certainly not the bulky craft in which they had commenced their odyssey.

"That should do it," announced Thompson, as he ejected the last pair of expended rockets, simultaneously extinguishing all remaining lights on the panel in front of him.

"Hallelujah!" voiced Chadwick, the geologist, among a background chatter of similar comments from several of his colleagues.

After their ordeal with multiple "G" forces the sudden absence of acceleration was a welcome relief. Other than a few relatively minor burns, necessitated by mid-course corrections, they would not have to undergo further stress from the force of gravity until insertion into Mars orbit. It still seemed strange to many people to learn that no additional thrust was needed to travel through space once escape velocity had been attained. But such was indeed the case, and all they had to do from now on was to quite literally coast to their destination.

Unstrapping themselves from their acceleration couches the crew of the Mars Voyager slowly arose and began flexing their limbs. Although adhesive shoes held them to specific sections designated as floors, they had to exercise some caution lest too vigorous movement send them flying into an unyielding bulkhead. Only in the four rotating wheel compartments could they partake of near normal muscular activity. On the whole, this unique ability to oscillate between two radically different gravitational states was definitely capable of preventing life from becoming dull.

Moving to the windows which encompassed the control center, the astronauts gazed in awe at the spectacle before them. Now filling much of their field of view, in a matter of hours the rapidly receding Earth would shrink to the size of a full Moon. In a few days it would be only an exceptionally bright planet. Two colors predominated. Endeavoring to compete with the deep blue ocean background were numerous white patches of cloud, along with the broad expanse of white marking Antarctica's polar ice cap. An outline of the African continent was clearly discernible, with the cloud-free Sahara Desert region exhibiting several shades of brown. Large portions of North and South America were also visible. Through rifts in the cloud cover the dark green of the Amazon River basin testified to the presence of vegetation.

"You can readily see how Africa and South America fit together like pieces in a jigsaw puzzle," Chadwick remarked. "If ever one needed visual confirmation of the drifting continent hypothesis, this view is surely it."

Not one of his companions felt inclined to disagree with him.

....

It was the evening following the much publicized departure of the Martian expedition. Professor Duncan was host to the three remaining members of the Thompson family. For at least the fourth time, the children were watching a TV replay of the Mars Voyager fading into the distance. The program soon ended and was promptly superseded by a soap commercial.

"Could we please have another astronomy lesson?" Robert asked, recalling a previous promise.

"I think it could be arranged," replied the professor. "As a matter of fact, the telescope is already set up and waiting."

Thankful for an exceptionally clear night sky, it was not long before the first image appeared on the TV screen. The magnificent spiral galaxy, known as M51, was the initial choice. Also named the Whirlpool Galaxy, it is believed to contain over 100 billion stars. At the end of one of the spiral arms was NGC 5195, a somewhat smaller companion system. Situated in the constellation of Canes Venatici, the two lay at a distance of roughly 25 million light-years, well outside the gravitational bond of our Local Group of galaxies. With a redshift of some 570 kilometers per second (km/s), M51 is assumed to share in a general expansion of the universe.

Conveying such statistics to his audience, the professor was pleased by the response. Asking the right questions, he well knew, is often the key to discovery.

"What do you think causes the universe to expand?" Robert wanted to know. "Is there a limit to the speed of a receding galaxy? Can it exceed the velocity of light?"

The professor answered: "The further astronomers probe into space the greater the implied velocities of recession. Virtually all evidence of expansion comes from a phenomenon referred to as a Doppler shift toward the red end of the spectrum. Essentially, it reflects the increased time of radiation propagation due to motion of recession. In turn, this movement acts to enhance wavelength. Based upon this reasoning, galaxies of the Ursa Major supercluster are revealed to be moving away at about 15,000 km/s. (A typical supercluster, which is believed to be the ultimate in clumping, may contain several thousand galaxies.) The more distant Corona Borealis supercluster is deduced to be receding at some 22,000 km/s; while the even more remote Hydra aggregation of galaxies has been measured at 61,000 km/s. Clusters at greater distances yield still higher velocities. Extrapolating this rate of recession to ever more distant systems, it may be computed that at a distance of approximately 18 billion light-years any galaxies will actually be rushing away from us at the velocity of light itself - some 300,000 km/s.

"With regard to the question of whether a material body can exceed the speed of light, it is really a matter of defining motion in terms of some universal point. Two galaxies located in opposite directions of the sky, for example, could be moving away from us at just under the speed of light. Relative to each other they would be receding at almost double the velocity of light. Hence, if there is some cosmic limitation of speed it must surely be in the form of motion relative to a common frame of reference - namely, *the very center of the universe!"*

"But what is the actual force or motivation behind this cosmic expansion?" asked an equally curious Janet.

Acknowledging that astronomers and cosmologists had proposed two fundamental creation models, in order to explain the phenomenon of an expanding universe, Professor Duncan proceeded to elaborate as follows:

"For quite some time the most acceptable cosmology, in the eyes of many scientists, has been the Big Bang theory of creation. According to this model the universe began with a truly stupendous explosion about 15 to 20 billion years ago. Flung outward from a common center, it is assumed that gravitation has succeeded in condensing matter into the stars and galaxies which we observe. However, in spite of its great popularity among members of the scientific community, this interpretation is beset by a number of serious faults. Upon a philosophical basis it will be seen to imply a transitory universe and (presumably) also a God which came into existence at this same instant. From a purely scientific aspect there is conflict with the logical assumption that gravity would compel matter to be condensed around centers of extreme mass. Instead, what is actually found is a peculiar 'honeycomb' distribution of galaxies, in which a large majority are situated around the edges of hollow spherical shells - with near voids at their centers! Rather than gravitation producing concentrated mass clumpings, like the globular clusters, we have a scenario indicative of *repulsion* beyond a certain point - a distance which is evidently of the order of some tens of millions of light-years. Also very difficult to reconcile with the Big Bang concept is the fact that quasars - conceded to be comparatively short-lived in terms of the inferred age of the universe - are observed more than a dozen billion light-years away (hence, at least this old), while others are still burning brightly relatively nearby. One would surely expect that these highly compacted objects would be formed not later than the first normal and less massive galaxies!

"The only conceivable alternative to an explosive origin is a principle known as Steady-state cosmology. In this model the universe is viewed as being infinite in time, as any matter lost through evolutionary processes is replenished by an equivalence of newly created hydrogen atoms between the clusters of galaxies. Lack of a mechanism with which to induce cosmic expansion, long considered a weak point in this theory, can readily be explained by postulating a *dual nature of gravitation.* In spite of all the so-called experts, it is my contention that the most plausible interpretation of evidence involves the premise of small-scale attraction combined with large-scale repulsion."

"Then you would conclude that the Big Bang model is probably wrong?" deduced Janet.

"Indubitably!" exclaimed the professor.

"I have always viewed this popular cosmology with suspicion," opined Erica. "It tended to relegate creation to a transitory and even obscure phenomenon; whereas the concept of a universe which embraced an Eternal Cosmic Principle made far more sense."

"I find cosmology to be just as fascinating as astronomy," Janet remarked.

"Indeed it is," agreed the professor. "Astronomical research is merely the means toward an end. Only when observation is woven into a coherent scheme does it begin to bear fruit - a fact often overlooked by many budding scientists who tend to become lost in trivia and fail to see the Big Picture."

"What I really find intriguing is the 'time machine' aspect of astronomical observation," ventured Erica. "I consider it quite remarkable that, upon viewing the heavens, one is actually dealing with celestial history."

"And very ancient history, in many instances," added Professor Duncan. "For the deeper man probes the depths of the universe, the further back into time he is reaching. Since all radiation is propagated at a finite velocity we see an object, not as it is at the moment we observe it, but as it was when this light commenced its journey. In the case of remote galactic systems this could be many millions (or even billions) of years ago. A galaxy which we now observe through our telescopes may not exist today! Only its ghostly image may survive in the form of tiny photons streaking through the vast expanse of space."

"How is it possible for light to approach us at the same rate of speed from galaxies receding at different velocities?" Robert inquired. "Our science teacher says that this is actually the case."

"I could never understand it either," chimed Susan. "It makes no sense to me at all."

The professor was fully aware of the strange paradox to which the children referred. Known as the "law of addition of speeds," this simple experience of everyday life is seemingly violated by radiation. In essence, it was the phenomenon whereby new motion is added to (or subtracted from) previous motion, so that velocity - relative to some common frame of reference - becomes the sum (plus or minus) of both velocities. For instance, if we expel a projectile from a moving object - in the direction of its motion - it will inherit any initial velocity in addition to this latest thrust. If ejected in the opposite direction its speed would, of course, simply be deducted. Until the classical light experiment of Michelson and Morley, in the year 1887, nobody ever questioned the validity of this firmly established physical law. When it was discovered that radiation always impacts at a constant velocity - independent of the motion of source or receiver - it promptly set the stage for a profound revolution in physics.

Unfortunately, to the dismay of Professor Duncan, events had managed to take a rather bizarre turn - in spite of the protests and doubts of a minority of highly qualified physicists. Instead of logically seeking an explanation in some as yet unexplored property of space, a preponderance of physicists and astronomers sought to circumvent the problem by ignoring the possibility that an unknown factor could act to regulate the speed of radiation. Thus it came to be accepted that the distance of a receding galaxy (in light-years) was also equal to the number of years that its light has spent in transit to us - quite regardless of the extra distance that source and receiver will cover during time needed for passage. The enigma of how radiation could leave one object and - rather magically - approach all others in its line of flight with the same velocity (regardless of whether they are approaching or receding), remained just that: *an unresolved mystery!*

Confronted with the spectacle of quasar redshifts with implied velocities well in excess of light speed, astronomers soon began to use a relativistic formula which reduced such motion to more plausible levels. Although appearing to solve one problem it did so at the expense of posing another. What was glossed over was the fact that this adopted formula really constituted a surreptitious reinstatement of the "law of addition of speeds" - a valid law of nature from which radiation was supposedly excluded so as to conform to the dictates of a misinterpreted light experiment! This radiation time/velocity paradox has yet to be resolved, and it continues to remain a distinct embarrassment to scientists who have failed to recognize many profound implications with regard to cosmology.

"I have always been opposed to solutions which involve the use of magic," said the professor. "From my earliest studies I could never accept the traditional concept of radiation propagation. I am convinced that science has been guilty of ignoring evidence and reason in order to avoid the consequences of supporting an obscure and erroneous interpretation."

"Have you formulated any theories as to how observation might be reconciled with common sense?" Janet asked.

"Yes I have," came the reply. "If the Steady-state creation model is valid, then the answer could very well lie in the manner in which radiation interacts with newly created matter forms in the depths of space. Although original ideas of the principle of continuous creation assumed that it took the form of hydrogen, the simplest atom and fundamental fuel of the stars, there is not the slightest reason why this should be so. It could certainly be of the nature of infinitesimal quanta - quanta many billions of times smaller than an electron. Such a scenario could explain a number of unresolved cosmic mysteries. The phenomenon of gravitation, for instance, could be the result of an exchange of these minute quanta - at essentially the speed of light - among the various material particles. Moreover, the interaction of radiation, with myriad swarms of these same elementary quanta, could account for a portion of the transit time observed as a redshift, since it is impossible for any physical reaction to occur in zero time."

"I see what you mean when you say that there are overlooked consequences," commented Erica.

"In particular, it could explain why so many nearby galaxies display redshifts instead of blueshifts, when their random motions should result in a much more equitable ratio," voiced Professor Duncan.

"What about radiation propagation and the expanding universe?" asked Janet. "How does this fit in with the idea of continuous creation?"

"One far-reaching consequence of radiation obeying the 'law of addition of speeds' involves the time factor," said the professor. "Of little importance at low velocities, the difference becomes enormous at high redshifts and recession velocities approaching the speed of light. In fact, it would require radiation transit times of many tens of billions of years in order to account for the redshifts of the more distant quasars. Most certainly, it would completely eliminate any form of Big Bang cosmology on the grounds of light transit time alone!"

"Do you think this could be the reason why so many astronomers are reluctant to reopen the issue of radiation propagation?" asked Robert, disproving any notion that the discussion was becoming too abstract for one his age.

"I rather suspect that this is indeed the case," replied the professor. "In my youth, I had always viewed scientists as a body dedicated to the impartial analysis of observational evidence, as opposed to religious zealots who rely solely upon blind faith. I now feel that I had very seriously overestimated the integrity of scientists in general. While there are undoubtedly many true and conscientious researchers in every branch of science, human pride can frequently color one's outlook. It is often just as difficult for a scientist - strongly committed to theory - to admit error, as it is for a priest to renounce his views and his vows."

"One can only hope that the scientific community will soon swallow its pride and initiate an unbiased assessment of crucial cosmological issues," philosophized Erica.

"Incidentally, a rather startling prediction must follow as a result of combining Steady-state cosmology with a revised concept of radiation propagation," announced the professor. "In order to conserve mass-energy, it is necessary to introduce a cosmic factor opposite to that of creation. In other words, for every atom that is created, so one must be annihilated. Were this not the case, the concept of a universe infinite in time would conflict with the idea of continuous creation - in the sense that it would imply a universe that is more than infinite in physical size!"

"How would you introduce this momentous factor?" asked Janet, more than a little intrigued.

"I can conceive of just one possibility," answered Professor Duncan. "Since expansion of the universe may only be reconciled with Steady-state cosmology by postulating a repulsive side to gravitation, a truly amazing thing must occur at the point where velocity of recession reaches the speed of light. In effect, as radiation strives to propagate toward the central regions of the universe, it will encounter an outward flow moving at the same velocity. In turn, this opposing flow must cancel any inward motion, producing a stationary energy field - one of absolutely staggering proportion as energy adds to energy within the framework of an eternal universe. In all essential respects, it may be likened unto an *encircling cosmic black hole!"*

"My God!" exclaimed Janet. "What happens when a planet or star system strikes this intense energy barrier?"

"Instant annihilation, I'm afraid," replied the professor.

"How far are we from this barrier?" Susan wanted to know.

"That is the big question! What I can tell you is that we reside in a highly eccentric position relative to the center of the universe," ventured the professor. "According to my study of quasars, with regard to distribution/luminosity/redshift, I have deduced that the nearby cosmic edge lies in the vicinity of the constellation Sculptor, in the Southern Hemisphere."

His audience left somewhat awed by such revelations, Professor Duncan returned to the computer console and punched in a series of new coordinates. A succession of images were projected on the TV screen. The last exterior system to be viewed was M87, a giant elliptical galaxy at the center of the Virgo cluster, roughly 50 million light-years distant. Much larger and more massive than our Milky Way, it was attended by thousands of globular clusters, some of which appeared as fuzzy patches of faint starlight.

"A dozen billion years ago this galaxy could well have been viewed as a quasar by a distant observer situated in some other supercluster," stated the professor.

"Does this mean that quasars evolve into galaxies?" Robert asked. "How are they formed?"

"Actually, quasars constitute the cores of very young and exceptionally massive galaxies, becoming less luminous with the passage of time. As for the question of origin, I think this is a subject which might best be deferred to some future date," said the professor, glancing at his wrist watch.

....

As month followed month the Mars Voyager continued to spiral outward from the Sun. Each day added several seconds to the time required for a radio message to reach Earth. By the time they reached Mars it would take close to six minutes for such impulses to cover the intervening distance. Precise measurement of the angle and time of transmission allowed Mission Control to monitor their progress with considerable accuracy.

Some two months into the journey it had been necessary for the astronauts to initiate a rocket burn with the liquid fuel engines. In making a mid-course correction it was really tantamount to a trade-off between precision and fuel efficiency. The longer they left the burn the more data would be available with which to plot their trajectory. On the other hand, the more they strayed off course the more fuel would be needed to rectify the error. Within the next three weeks a second and somewhat shorter burn was made. Tracking experts on Earth had been unanimous in their belief that no further corrections would be required before igniting a series of solid fuel rockets in a major deceleration program - one that was designed to cut their speed and allow capture by the Martian gravitational field.

While far from the most fuel efficient of plans, the use of batteries of solid fuel rockets permitted the luxury of simply adding enough of them to provide the necessary thrust. At the expense of expending more fuel it had permitted them to reach Mars in little more than three months. Allowing for a stay of not more than one month in the vicinity of the Red Planet, it would take the adventurers almost six months to catch up with a now receding Earth. Ten months was certainly preferable to adopting the most fuel efficient trip possible, which would have taken something like 31 months!

During the three long months that the Mars Voyager had been hurtling through space the crew had remained in good spirits. The ability to oscillate between contrasting states of weightlessness and artificial gravity did much to preserve physical fitness in an unnatural environment. Regularly scheduled exercise on the treadmill, bicycle, and an assortment of spring-type apparatus, kept their muscles in proper tone. Nor were their minds allowed to deteriorate. Through the use of sophisticated computer/video technology they were able to simulate a variety of situations that required fast reaction and intelligent response. Not one of the astronauts felt inclined to take these simulations lightly, since their lives could very easily be jeopardized by a careless and inappropriate decision.

Recreation consisted of a generous selection of music discs and video tapes. Friendly chess and card games also played a role in relieving any boredom which arose during their spare time. The expedition's appointed leader, Boris Brodsky, was soon conceded to be the ship's chess wizard. The best that any of his companions could do was a draw, and only geologist Martin Chadwick managed that feat at the expense of five losses. However, his American opponent felt that he had learned a great deal in the course of this humiliation. Perhaps, he thought, on the return voyage he might catch the Russian off guard and eke out at least one win.

The astronauts were now so close to their destination that they could clearly see many surface features with the naked eye. A white polar cap stood out in marked contrast to the reddish-brown surface, permeated in places with a number of dark blotches and rifts. Completely absent was any trace of blue oceans and green vegetation. With a mass just a little over 10% that of Earth, there were two characteristics that it did have in common with its closest neighbor. First, the Martian day was a scant 37 minutes longer. Second, the inclination of its equator (with respect to orbit) was less than two degrees greater. This last statistic assured the planet of four seasons as on Earth, except that its year was something like 687 of our days.

A sudden announcement came over the ship's intercom system, instructing all crew members to prepare for immediate deceleration and insertion into Mars orbit. The big craft was gradually turned until properly oriented. The moment was at hand when they would again experience multiple "G" forces.

"Everybody ready?" Brodsky asked, adjusting the position of his reclining seat.

Satisfied that his companions were firmly strapped in, Brodsky then gave the signal to initiate the prescribed firing sequence. Jammed deep into their acceleration couches, the seven adventurers were relieved when the last ignited solid fuel rocket burned out and was subsequently ejected into space. With relative velocity cut to under 5 km/s they would soon be captured by the planet's gravitational field. Henceforth, any refinement of orbit would be achieved through a series of short burns with the craft's liquid fuel engines. "I guess we can let Mission Control know that we've just gone into Mars orbit," a jubilant Yamoto finally announced, glancing up from the radar screen which he had been carefully monitoring.

Beaming the news back to Earth, the explorers knew that any reply could not be expected for at least another twelve minutes. Meanwhile, there was no reason why they should not enjoy the truly spectacular view now visible through the windows of their bridge control center.

Chapter 3

AMAZING DISCOVERY

Although the astronauts had no intention of visiting either pole, there was a degree of flexibility in entering into a polar orbit around Mars. In short, it allowed them to select a landing site anywhere on the Martian surface, as the planet's rotation would carry them over a different region with each cycle. Simple adjustment in the size of their orbit would afford a convenient descent window, during which a chosen site would lie directly in the path of their motion. As planned, they were currently in an elliptical trajectory which took them within 1,000 kilometers (km) of the surface at point of closest approach; while at apogee the distance was slightly in excess of 10,000 km. One full circuit about Mars required a little over seven hours.

Common knowledge since the days of the first Mariner space probe, the surface of the Red Planet could be classified into several types of areas. Other than the frozen polar caps, there were two rather contrasting regions: plains, which dominate much of the northern half of the planet; and rough, impact cratered terrain, which covers most of the south. Constituting close to 40% of the Martian surface, the plains may be described in terms of low-elevation regions largely buried by old lava flows. The remaining surface area consisted primarily of abundantly cratered highlands. Tharsis, one of the highland areas, extends over very nearly a quarter of the entire surface of the planet, and averages a height of some 6 km above the mean surface level. This ancient and rather extensive plateau is thought, by many specialists in planetary geology, to be the Martian equivalent of Earth's great continents. With a diameter of almost 6,800 km (4,200 miles), the surface area of Mars becomes comparable to our own planet's total land mass.

Clearly visible to an astronaut's naked eye was a row of three giant volcanoes on the Tharsis highland dome. Known as Ascraeus Mons, Pavonis Mons and Arsia Mons, these volcanoes are far larger than any which exist on Earth. Spaced some 700 km apart, they straddled the Martian equator on a line stretching from southwest to northeast. Generally believed to have been active between 100 and 700 million years ago, they had almost certainly lain dormant for long periods of time. In all probability, their great size had much to do with the lack of continental drift on Mars, since any movement away from the underlying hot spots (which had created them) would have precluded such a prodigious outpouring of lava material. This absence of tectonic activity was thought to be consistent with the planet's exceedingly weak magnetic field, and implied that Mars may not possess a fluid core. It was also an indication that its surface crust is probably quite thick and was formed in a relatively short period of time.

However, the monster of all Solar System volcanoes lay about 1,200 km to the northwest of this giant trio. Olympus Mons, which rose some 25 km (15 miles) into the Martian sky, rested on a base that extended a staggering 600 km (400 miles) across! The seven crew members aboard the Mars Voyager were awed by the thought that one volcano could cover an area the size of the entire state of Colorado. Crowning the top of this mammoth structure was a large depressed basin or crater some 65 km in diameter, long filled with solidified lava. For decades the experts had speculated as to when the last major lava flow had taken place. If one suggested figure of several tens of millions of years was correct, it raised the possibility that a small amount of activity might still occur from time to time. At every opportunity the astronauts planned to observe this interesting site through the ship's telescope.

Yet another remarkable feature to be viewed was an enormous rift valley, stretching some 4,500 km (2,800 miles) across the central region of the planet. Named Valles Marineris, in honor of the Mariner 9 probe which first revealed its existence, this great chasm averages more than 200 km across (about 700 km at its widest point) and 7 km deep at its deepest. Formed by a major faulting of the crust some billions of years ago - most probably when the Tharsis highland was uplifted - it is large enough to be viewed as a dark marking through Earth based telescopes. Without a doubt, it completely dwarfed the Grand Canyon in every respect.

One additional marking visible from Earth is an immense lava-filled impact crater known as Hellas. This circular basin is some 1,800 km (1,100 miles) wide, and stands as mute testimony to the violent era of asteroid body collisions which marked the planet's early history. Its floor, believed to be the lowest point on Mars, lay some 5 km (3 miles) below an already depressed region. In spite of the thin Martian atmosphere, morning mists had often been observed here, as was the case with respect to a number of other low-lying regions.

While considerably less spectacular than the great rift of Valles Marineris, the Martian surface exhibited numerous winding and branching channels, which gave one the distinct impression of dried-up river beds. Since there was obviously no water flowing on the surface today, their presence had raised the question as to what could have happened to all this liquid water. Adding to the mystery was the revelation that many of these channels did not actually flow from high elevations into depressed basins, such as ancient sea beds. Instead, they appeared to quite literally burst out of the ground and flow much like a sudden flood over adjoining terrain. Whatever the explanation (i.e. volcanic heating or heat from asteroid impacts), it seemed a virtual certainty that Mars once possessed substantial quantities of water.

Acknowledging this fact, many scientists soon concluded that some of this water must still exist in the form of permafrost beneath the surface. Assuming that both Mars and Earth initially had a similar ratio of primordial water to other ingredients, the factor of mass stands as the only real difference to which one might appeal in order to resolve the "missing water" puzzle. The weaker Martian gravity, according to a promising theory, would be less able to contain water vaporized into the atmosphere. Since extreme heat would more readily dissipate the hydrogen component into space, it would leave behind large amounts of free oxygen which could be expected to combine with other crustal elements. Thus the planet's reddish-brown color may well be due, in large measure, to iron oxide (rust) produced by oxygen derived from dissociated water molecules. In any event, there was a general consensus of opinion, among the experts, that the astronauts stood a very good chance of finding water in underground reservoirs of permafrost.

Water certainly existed in a frozen state at the poles, often in conjunction with quantities of dry ice (frozen carbon dioxide). This much had been determined as far back as the days of the Viking orbiters, when it was discovered that summertime heat left a white residual after temperatures passed the point where frozen carbon dioxide would be vaporized. Moreover, from the amount of water vapor detected with the orbiter's spectograph, it seemed rather safe to conclude that water ice must constitute the noted residual. Just how thick this icy coating might be had yet to be determined.

While atmospheric pressure at the planet's surface was only about 1% that on Earth (equivalent to an altitude of some 30 km), it was sufficient to permit the formation of sporadic layers of thin cloud cover. Consisting of some 95% carbon dioxide and 2.7% nitrogen, with traces of other gases, the Martian atmosphere also contained variable quantities of water vapor. During the summer season levels of this vital commodity could actually reach a few percent, making it possible to form white clouds of ice crystals. Such clouds are to be found in lowlands in the early morning, and in regions where winds force the air up mountain slopes, causing any water vapor to cool and condense. Extensive cloud cover may also be observed over each polar cap with the advent of respective summers.

The tenuous Martian atmosphere was quite capable of supporting dust storms. In fact, when the Mariner 9 orbital space probe (of 1971) reached Mars it was stymied for several months by a great dust storm which covered much of the planet. Produced by uneven heating and cooling of the surface - due to a variety of daily, seasonal and orbital fluctuations - strong winds are a frequent occurrence. Although the extreme thinness of the atmosphere could reduce a 200 km per hour hurricane to little more than a gentle breeze, in terms of a wind on Earth, it was nevertheless capable of lifting fine grains of sand and dust, and to distribute it over a considerable area. The mystery of why many surface features were observed to change in intensity and shape, from year to year, turned out to be the result of covering or uncovering regions of lighter or darker rock by windblown dust. Wedge-shaped Syrtis Major, the most prominent of all the changing dark areas on the planet, was revealed to be a gradual descending slope situated to the west of an impact cratered highland region.

During the four days that the adventurers had been in Mars orbit, they had once come within 10,000 km of Phobos, largest of the planet's two moons. An irregular object, measuring roughly 27 km long by 19 km wide, it was suspected by many astronomers of being a captured asteroid. What really served to draw attention, however, was the presence of a relatively large crater (some 10 km across) named Stickney. How could an impact, sufficient to form a crater this size, fail to shatter the entire body? Had the impact occurred prior to the birth of Phobos when, conceivably, this moon was still part of a more massive primordial body - one which was subsequently broken up when struck by another sizable asteroid? More than one astronaut expressed regret that mission plans did not include a visit to this intriguing object. Orbiting above the Red Planet's surface, at an average distance of about 6,000 km, Phobos is observed to complete one revolution in a period of some 7 hours and 40 minutes.

Deimos, the other Martian satellite, was discovered (along with its companion) in 1877, and is somewhat smaller and more distant than Phobos. Measuring approximately 13 km in diameter, it orbits the planet's surface at an average distance of about 20,000 km, completing one revolution in a period of roughly 30 hours. Like all moons locked in a close gravitational embrace with a much more massive primary body, both Deimos and Phobos had long ceased to rotate as such and continued to present the same side toward Mars.

The moment was fast approaching when orbital momentum would place the astronauts in a favorable position for a descent to the prescribed landing site on the Martian surface. Their target was a promising location in the vicinity of the southeast corner of a region known as Acidalia Planitia. The "Face" itself lay in the adjoining desert area of Cydonia, at the coordinates of 41 degrees N latitude and 9.5 degrees W longitude. This enigmatic structure was situated some 1,200 km NE of the site where Earth's Viking 1 lander made its historic touchdown on July 20, 1976. The eastern edge of the prominent Valles Marineris canyon complex lay over 2,000 km to the south and west of their intended base.

Some four hours earlier the five chosen crew members (Brodsky, Thompson, Chadwick, Walker, Lin) had transferred from the mother ship to the Explorer landing vehicle. Following a quick systems check, all seemed to be in order and separation of the two craft had proceeded on schedule and according to plan.

"Prepare to initiate rocket burn on my signal," announced Brodsky, watching the seconds wind down on the computer screen directly in front of him.

"Ready," Thompson responded, placing his finger on the switch which would ignite the single solid fuel rocket that was capable of taking them out of orbit and sending their ship plunging toward the surface more than a thousand kilometers below.

"Now!" Brodsky commanded.

An orange tongue of flame shot forward in the direction of their motion. Coinciding with this surge of thrust was a return of the sense of gravity, which pushed the adventurers deep into their padded seats. The Mars Voyager, visible before only a few hundred meters away, suddenly appeared to shoot ahead of them at a steadily increasing pace. In mere seconds it was completely lost to sight. Within a minute the rocket burned out and was promptly ejected. From this point on deceleration would be accomplished by means of their two liquid fuel engines, a built-in heat shield, and a specially designed drag-chute.

Aerobraking with the heat shield was the first to be utilized, as they entered the top layers of the tenuous Martian atmosphere. Barely perceptible at first, deceleration soon became pronounced as the Explorer dropped lower and the air grew thicker. A series of short rocket burns kept them on their intended trajectory, as well as serving to reduce forward motion. At an altitude of just over twelve thousand meters the drag-chute was deployed. By the time they had dropped to four thousand meters their descent rate had fallen to little more than three hundred kilometers per hour. Still, the surface seemed to be rushing toward them at enormous speed.

"We're heading straight for a sizable impact crater," Thompson warned, peering at the image projected on his video screen.

"Twenty-five degree clockwise rotation!" responded Brodsky, as he prepared to take evasive action.

"A six second burn at one-quarter thrust should do the trick," advised Thompson.

"Initiate prescribed burn upon reaching one-zero-two," Brodsky ordered, satisfied that this correction would carry them well away from the obstacle now in their path.

Twin tongues of flame soon changed the angle of their fall, and it was not long before they were descending over a relatively flat landscape at an altitude of one thousand meters. Following an orientation maneuver, after negating much of their lateral motion, the main thrusters were aligned almost vertically with respect to the Martian surface and the drag-chute was finally cut loose, its function now fulfilled.

"Descent speed forty meters per second....Forward motion 1.5 meters per second....Altitude eight hundred meters," announced Thompson.

"Ten percent throttle," called Brodsky. "We'll hold briefly at a hundred meters in order to get a clear look at the surface."

"Eight percent fuel remaining," advised Thompson.

"Looking good," added Chadwick. "Very few rocks over one meter are visible."

"Take us straight down....Five percent thrust," called out Brodsky.

"Kicking up dust," said Chadwick, as the TV image suddenly began to blur.

"Descent two meters per second....Altitude twenty meters.... Forward speed negligible," remarked Thompson, his eyes riveted to the radar altimeter.

The Explorer landing module hovered momentarily some twelve meters above the surface. Eventually, after a last subdued gasp of rocket exhaust, it settled to the ground amidst a cloud of disturbed sand and dust. Feeling only a modest jolt, as the shock-absorbing legs of the craft did their job, the astronauts welcomed the silence and lack of vibration when the propulsion system shut down. For better or for worse, man had managed to reach the surface of the Red Planet in safety.

Unable to immediately contact the Mars Voyager, which was presently on the other side of the planet, the five joyous crew members proceeded to exude words of congratulation on behalf of the historic occasion. It had been a long trip and they could hardly wait to set foot on solid ground again.

With curiosity prevailing, the adventurers found themselves drawn to the windows encompassing the upper stage control center. Fortunately, the dust had now settled and no longer obscured their view. They gazed upon a truly desolate scene of gently rolling sand dunes, replete with a modest number of scattered rocks and boulders. In the opposite direction they could see much rougher terrain. Along with several sizable impact craters were distant hills and valleys, which marked the location of one of their prime objectives: a suspected dried-up river bed region that featured winding canyons and outflow channels.

Eventually establishing communication with the orbiting mother ship, news of their successful landing was received with a great deal of relief - both aboard the Mars Voyager and, some minutes later, by an anxious Mission Control back on Earth. In due time, the various news media responded by proclaiming the expedition to be on the verge of a new era in the saga of mankind. (There was simply no way to foretell the magnitude of the discoveries and events that were to follow.)

With barely three hours of daylight remaining, it was decided to postpone their grand exit from the Explorer until the following morning. Refreshed and rested after a good night's sleep, they would be better prepared for what promised to be a very busy day. Even so, it was difficult for them to resist the urge to charge outside and plant their feet firmly upon the soil of this alien planet. But patience, being an essential ingredient in molding an astronaut, managed to prevail and the temptation was suppressed.

However, the issue of setting foot on the Martian surface did raise one question: Who would be first? By unanimous consent it was agreed to cut a deck of playing cards, with high man receiving the honor of being the first human to place his footprint upon the soil of the Red Planet. With one exception, the person drawing the lowest card would have to remain aboard the Explorer in order to monitor communications. This exception was physicist Chou Lin, whose expertise would be needed to set up their portable nuclear reactor.

"Five of clubs," declared Boris Brodsky, the first crew member to select a card.

"Four of hearts," conceded a rather pessimistic Adam Thompson, picking second.

"Queen of spades," announced a smiling Martin Chadwick, noting that his card was well above the average.

"Nine of clubs," said Chou Lin.

"King of diamonds!" exclaimed a jubilant Jeffery Walker, the expedition's physician/microbiologist.

"At least we didn't succumb to Boris' suggestion to decide the matter by means of a chess tournament," remarked Thompson, long resigned to the fact that he would be the last of the five to make a grand entrance come morning.

Dawn, when it did arrive, bathed the landscape with a pinkish glow. Produced by a combination of suspended fine dust particles and a rust colored surface, it was a view that quite pervaded the senses. There was a general feeling that the total absence of blue and green - so common on Earth in the form of water, sky and vegetation - would ultimately prove dull and boring, if not even depressing.

Spirits, however, were high as the four chosen astronauts made ready to exit the Explorer. Adorned in their protective space suits, they bade goodbye to their remaining colleague and promptly descended into the air lock. Located at the center of what was now the floor of the crew compartment, it led downward into the lower stage. Closing the hatch behind them, they proceeded to activate the dual pumps which would transfer the chamber's air into a nearby holding tank. In little more than a minute the pressure was reduced to that of the thin Martian atmosphere and the pumps cut off. Opening an opposing hatch, they entered a spacious cylindrical tube and commenced their descent down a built-in ladder, the air lock door closing automatically behind them. Upon reaching the top of the lower stage they made a slight detour around the exhaust nozzle of the ascent module, which was designed to fire through this same passageway.

"I'd sure hate to climb this ladder in full Earth gravity," remarked Chadwick. "These heavy suits would appear to weigh a ton."

A chorus of assenting voices could be heard over their radio link, highlighted by Walker's comment: "A forty pound burden is certainly preferable to lugging around one weighing well over a hundred."

Reaching the bottom of the shaft, Brodsky pushed a series of buttons on a small control panel. In response, a section of the floor began to open up and swing downward, producing a moderately curved ramp that was inclined some thirty degrees to the Martian surface which lay below.

"So far so good," opined Walker. "Is the video camera ready to record my grand exit?"

"I suppose your first act will be to pick up a rock and see how far you can throw it in the weak gravity of this planet," chided Chadwick.

"Nothing quite so dramatic," responded Walker. "I think a simple wave to my billion plus audience should suffice."

"I have a better idea," interjected Brodsky. "Why don't we hand our celebrity a video camera? Not only could he give us a first person view of man's initial footsteps, but he would then be in position to tape us deploying the Mars Rover."

"It's a deal," said Walker. "You tape me and I'll tape your caper with the tractor."

Within the span of the next forty minutes the adventurers had succeeded in winching the Rover down to the planet's surface. In similar fashion, the portable nuclear reactor was also lowered and safely shielded behind a clump of nearby boulders. It was not long before physicist Chou Lin had it operating and delivering much needed electrical power to the Explorer through a connecting cable. Should this vital energy source ever fail, the bitterly cold Martian nights would spell finish to their intended plans for exploration. Although still not exactly mild, as the Sun climbed higher in the sky the temperature continued to rise, eventually surpassing the freezing point of water.

During the course of the first day a wealth of video images was beamed by Thompson to the orbiting Mars Voyager, from whence it was promptly relayed to a captive audience back on Earth. For the best part of a month an unprecedented number of TV viewers would be treated to a daily report of events, highlighted by a series of remarkable images provided by a camera mounted on top of the Rover.

By the end of the second week the explorers had made two very significant discoveries. Utilizing a portable drilling apparatus, at the site of a suspected dried-up ancient river channel, water was found in the form of permafrost at a depth of twelve meters. The other discovery was made by Walker, who caused quite a stir among members of the scientific community. Upon subjecting some rock specimens to microscopic analysis, he came across irrefutable fossil evidence of primitive Martian life. What appeared to be a type of blue-green algae, of a complexity not too dissimilar to that of simple Earth strains, was revealed embedded in rocks which were estimated to be at least three billion years old. Biological life, it would seem, had actually begun on Mars just prior to the time that it had commenced on its closest planetary neighbor. As the now famous microbiologist hastened to point out in one of his TV reports, however, widely differing surface conditions must have terminated normal evolutionary processes on Mars long before the development of higher life forms.

With barely more than one week available for any additional exploration, their secondary objective was now the chief topic of discussion. An expedition to the controversial "Face" could no longer be put off. While previous excursions with the Mars Rover had been restricted to day trips, a journey to this relatively distant rock formation would entail an overnight stay. It would also tax the endurance of both man and machine. Although their vehicle was pressurized and heavily insulated, with a limited supply of electrical power it could offer the crew little in the way of heat during the bitterly cold Martian night. Situated as they were almost 200 km from the "Face," it was calculated that a round trip to this peculiar formation would leave them with only a small reservoir of energy. All factors considered, it had to be conceded that the proposed journey was not without a definite measure of risk. Indeed, should a serious malfunction occur, at such a great distance from their base, the prognosis would be rather grim.

In order to conserve weight and avoid any needless risk of personnel, it was decided that only two crew members would make the trip. Martin Chadwick, the geologist, was an obvious choice to study the structure of the "Face." After some deliberation it was finally agreed that Adam Thompson would pilot the Rover, which now awaited them with fully recharged batteries. It promised to be the drive of their lives for the two astronaut/motorists.

The vehicle itself would draw its power from three sources. Along with an extra complement of storage batteries, it carried an ingenious device known as a fuel cell. This unit was capable of combining oxygen with hydrogen to form drinking water, with a most important by-product being the generation of electricity. Another supplement to their power supply was a cluster of solar panels which covered the entire roof of the Rover. It was anticipated that this additional contribution, while admittedly small, would afford enough power to assure success of the mission. In a very short period of time this faith would be put to the test.

Armed with a detailed map of the intervening terrain, and with their course carefully plotted, the two adventurers bade farewell to their comrades and entered the tiny air lock of the Mars Rover. Cycling through to the pressurized interior, they removed their bulky space suits and seated themselves before a control console containing a surprising number of dials and switches. Running through a check list, they opened a radio link to the Explorer.

"See you guys sometime tomorrow afternoon," said Thompson, satisfied that all was in order.

"Have a good trip," came Brodsky's voice over the vehicle's speaker.

"You forgot to tell us what to do if we run into a bunch of little green men," Chadwick jested.

"Just don't antagonize them," advised Walker. "Remember, we didn't bring any firearms."

"If they appear unfriendly don't let on that you have chums sitting here in a defenseless spacecraft," added Chou Lin.

Amidst such banter the Mars Rover began to move forward, its caterpillar treads churning up a cloud of dust and sand. In a few short minutes it passed over a hilltop and was lost to sight to observers aboard the Explorer.

Navigation would be accomplished by means of their gyrocompass and a series of distinguishing landmarks charted in detail on a high resolution photo/map. Periodically, they would be able to establish communication with the orbiting Mars Voyager, permitting an accurate assessment of their progress. With a cruising speed of 30 km per hour it would likely take close to seven hours to reach their objective, assuming no complications or necessity to detour.

Painted a brilliant yellow, the Rover exhibited a high profile as it plodded across the Martian landscape. Out of contact with the Explorer, they welcomed every opportunity to vocalize with Maladev and Yamoto on board the mother ship. According to the latest radio fix they were now close to the halfway point in their journey. As planned, they had just finished beaming highlights of the trip up to their orbiting colleagues, where it would soon be featured on all of Earth's major TV networks. So far all had gone smoothly and they were right on schedule.

However, it was almost inevitable that some difficulty would arise. Shortly after concluding their last communication with the Mars Voyager they encountered a region containing large numbers of boulders, forcing them to adopt a somewhat zigzag course. Before long it was evident that their present path could lead them into trouble. Indeed, they were in danger of finding themselves boxed into a dead end situation between the steep walls of two sizable impact craters.

"I don't like the looks of this at all," remarked Thompson, shifting uneasily in the driver's seat.

"I'm forced to agree," Chadwick conceded. "Do you think we should back up and try another route?"

"Let's have a look at the map," replied Thompson, bringing the Rover to a full stop in front of what seemed to be an impenetrable barrier of scattered rocks and boulders.

"It has many aspects of a giant maze," opined his companion.

"We could certainly waste a lot of precious time and power in trying to find a way through this chaotic region. How much longer would it be to go around the twin craters?" asked Thompson.

"About twenty kilometers, I should think," answered Chadwick, after some deliberation.

"Damn! A bypass is going to take a huge bite out of our very meager battery reserves."

Chadwick immediately began to punch data into the vehicle's computer. Finally, he said: "We can still make it; but it'll be cutting things pretty fine."

"I really can't see any alternative," sighed Thompson, as he very reluctantly proceeded to put the Rover into reverse. "I sure hope we don't run into another impasse like this one."

"Our best bet is to bypass the craters to the right," advised Chadwick. "The landscape seems much flatter and less likely to be strewn with boulders. Unfortunately, there is a small outflow channel branch which we may have to go around in order to get back on course."

"Give me the worst case scenario."

"About five or six kilometers, I should say."

"If it's any further we may have to get out and push. Don't forget that this extra distance will have to be multiplied by two for a return trip," Thompson warned.

As events turned out, they were able to find a way across the meandering depression with only a minor detour. In terms of time this unforeseen setback had cost the explorers more than an hour of valuable daylight. It also cut deeply into their very limited reserve of electrical power, raising the prospect of having to abort the mission should additional obstacles be encountered.

Some three hours later optimism began to replace pessimism. They had finally broken into the clear and were presently making good time churning across relatively benign terrain, punctuated now and then with only modest impact craters, eroded hills and small mountain remnants. While scattered rocks and boulders still caused them a measure of concern, they did not appear to pose a serious problem.

"How much further?" asked Thompson, casting a watchful eye on a cluster of instruments.

"We should be able to catch a glimpse of it any moment now," replied Chadwick. "According to my calculations we can't be more than seven or eight kilometers away."

"I sure hope so, our power supply is fast becoming critical. Say, isn't that escarpment on the right our last check point?"

"Affirmative," Chadwick answered, glancing at the map beside him. "Turn right about 25 degrees once we pass over that rise ahead of us."

Exactly four minutes later their objective loomed large on the horizon. Somehow, it did not seem especially interesting. As a matter of fact, at first sight it looked just like one of the many rock formations they had already passed. However, as they drew closer it had to be conceded that it did seem to bear a strong resemblance to the silhouette of a human head.

With the TV camera activated, they approached to within a few hundred meters of the peculiar structure and came to a full stop. Much as they would have liked to make a complete circuit of the "Face" before exploring on foot, it was a luxury of another six kilometers that their dwindling power supply could ill afford.

"End of the line. All passengers out," announced Thompson, rising from his seat and flexing stiff muscles.

"Hallelujah!" exclaimed Chadwick. "I must confess that there was a time when I didn't think we would make it."

"Ditto," came the reply.

"Communication with the Mars Voyager should be possible in about ten minutes. Why don't we grab a bite to eat before getting down to business?" Chadwick suggested.

"Excellent idea," responded Thompson. "I'm famished."

A scant forty minutes elapsed before two space-suited figures emerged from the Rover's air lock. Having first informed their orbiting colleagues of their arrival, and refreshed after a hasty meal, they strove to make full use of the precious few hours of remaining daylight.

"Do you think we'll be able to find a way to climb to the top of this weird formation?" Thompson asked, opening the hatch to the unpressurized storage compartment at the rear of their vehicle.

"Good question. A close examination of the so-called facial features would certainly prove helpful."

Along with geologist tools and sample bags, the two explorers removed a length of strong nylon rope and climbing paraphernalia. Although given a crash course on certain fundamentals of mountain climbing, they were under strict orders to avoid unnecessary risk, as agility and a cumbersome space suit were far from synonymous. Thus equipped, they moved toward the enigmatic "Face."

Reaching the base of the cliff they began to search for a way up. Since the "chin" region was close to a vertical wall, they proceeded to look in the opposite direction. According to photos, their best bet seemed to lie in the vicinity of the left "eye," which was less than one kilometer from where they now stood. As they trudged along the periphery of the structure they could not help noticing a number of dual converging gouges on the side of the eroded escarpment.

"Strange series of horizontal grooves," remarked Thompson. "What do you think could have caused them?"

"Damned if I know," responded the geologist. "I must confess that I have never seen anything quite like this. The pattern is not consistent with normal stress fracturing."

"It's hard to say how deep they are. They seem to form an evenly spaced intermittent line about seven meters above ground level," observed Thompson.

"Unfortunately, they're too high to reach without performing heroics," lamented Chadwick. "But what really intrigues me is that the grooves are not parallel. They all tend to converge toward a point."

"And in all the same direction," added Thompson.

But the mystery of the highly elongated "V" shaped gouges was soon replaced by another peculiarity. Having reached a position immediately below the "eye," they gazed upward at what appeared to be a sloping pathway leading toward the summit.

"This could be easier than we thought," reasoned Chadwick.

"I'm glad something is going right at last," said Thompson, starting up the narrow trail.

Almost to the top, they encountered a minor snag in the form of debris which had evidently fallen from above. A large boulder effectively blocked their passage, stopping them dead in their tracks.

"You know, I think I could climb over this accursed rock if you would give me a boost," ventured Chadwick, after studying the situation. "There's a small fissure where I should be able to drive in a metal spike. One firm handhold would be all I need."

Ten minutes later, following the prescribed method of attack, Thompson allowed himself to be pulled up and over the obstacle. With his companion at the other end of a rope, the climb had been relatively easy. He was pleasantly surprised at how proficiently the geologist had managed the task.

"You never told me you were such a good mountain climber," said Thompson, as the two resumed their ascent.

"In my younger days I used to do it as a weekend sport. But I must admit that I never dreamed the skill would prove so useful."

Upon reaching the summit they moved directly to a nearby "eye" and peered into the oval crater. Characterized by walls that were of moderate slope, it was about 30 meters deep.

As he lowered his companion by rope, Thompson found himself pondering the unusual shape of the crater. "How many oval craters have you ever seen?" he finally asked over their radio link.

"None so extreme," Chadwick was forced to concede. "By the

way, Adam, make sure you have a good grip on the rope, as this surface is incredibly slippery. In fact, underneath a coating of dust and sand it appears to be like glass!"

"Do you think it's the result of a meteorite impact?"

"Such heat has been known to fuse certain rocks into glass," replied the geologist, chipping out a sample with his hammer and placing it into a plastic bag.

In due course the right "eye" was investigated in similar fashion. For all intents and purposes, it appeared to be a good duplicate of the first. The prospect of finding two exceedingly rare oval impact craters, separated by only a few hundred meters, became a topic of conversation.

"What do you think the odds are of two meteorites striking at such a highly oblique angle?" Thompson asked.

"Actually, it's not quite the fluke you might think. While pairs of gravitationally entwined asteroid/meteorite bodies are certainly the exception, they are not that uncommon," replied Chadwick. "If one could strike at an extreme angle, so would its twin."

"Let's have a look at the other so-called facial features," suggested Thompson.

Moving over to the raised area that passed for a "nose," they were again struck by a remarkable coincidence, as the protrusion was situated in an anatomically correct location and of just the right proportion. Even the two small cavities which could be construed to be "nostrils" seemed to be fortuitously placed.

"Damndest thing!" exclaimed Chadwick, securing yet another sample for later analysis.

Proceeding to the "mouth" region, they were confronted with an even greater mystery. The very outline of the depression defied explanation. There was virtually no way they could account for its shape through meteorite impact. The more they thought about it the more baffled they became.

"If I hadn't seen it with my own eyes I swear that I wouldn't have believed it," remarked Thompson, clearly awed by the scene before them.

"It sure looks like the work of a master sculptor," agreed the geologist, noting that the same glass-like surface lay beneath varying depths of wind-blown fine sand.

Finishing their video taping of the various facial features, the two began their downward trek to ground level. There was now little more than a couple of hours of daylight remaining, and they still had a lot of exploring to do.

"You know, Martin, I've been wondering if this convenient pathway to the summit is just another coincidence."

"How many remarkable coincidences do you want in one day?" responded Chadwick, at a loss for anything better to say.

Engrossed in such thoughts they reached the bottom of the "Face" and resumed their circumnavigation of the formation. For over a kilometer they noted nothing unusual, other than that of the peculiar grooves, which went on as before. At this point they made a discovery. Quite abruptly, and for no reason that they could discern, the converging gouges reversed polarity! As far as the eye could see, they were all oriented in this new and opposite direction.

"What do you make of this latest peculiarity?" asked Thompson.

"You're asking me? I haven't begun to figure out any of the previous mysteries."

Continuing their exploration they traveled an estimated two kilometers before reaching the region of the "chin," where they noticed a marked change in the pattern of the enigmatic grooves. Instead of lying horizontal, they suddenly pointed straight down! Curious as to how far these vertical gouges extended, they decided to trudge onward. In short order, the vertical markings ended and were replaced by horizontal grooves, so oriented as to converge in the same clockwise direction as originally noted. A few hundred meters later the reversed pattern had not changed.

"We're now back to square one," declared Thompson. "This is the point where we began."

"Unless I'm mistaken," said Chadwick, "the two reversals of polarity occur at opposite ends of this strange rock formation."

"You're quite right; the reversals are diametrically opposed. But why should one reversal point be characterized by vertical grooves?" Thompson wanted to know.

"Good question. Why don't we go back and have another look? It's not very far."

Agreeing with his comrade's suggestion, the two started back toward the "chin." Upon reaching the center of the mysterious vertical grooves they paused and carefully surveyed the markings, recording the scene in some detail with their video camera. As they did so a thought occurred to them.

"Do you notice how much lower these weird vertical grooves are situated on the rock face?" Thompson asked. "Moreover, the closer one gets to the center of this cluster of grooves the closer they extend toward the ground."

"I see what you mean. If we weren't standing so close to the cliff wall the whole pattern would resemble a gigantic arrowhead pointing downward."

"Exactly! It's almost as if we're looking at some sort of treasure map - with the treasure buried directly beneath this big arrow," suggested Thompson.

"That's kind of a wild interpretation," voiced the geologist, not wanting to let himself be carried away with the idea.

"I have to admit it does seem rather far-fetched," Thompson readily conceded. "But look at this one especially long groove; it even extends below ground level."

"Actually, there is a great deal of sand piled up against the rock face. The real surface is probably several meters lower."

"Why don't we try digging away some of this drifted sand?" Thompson urged.

"Seems a bit crazy to me, but I'm game. Just don't mention this caper to any of our fellow astronauts if we fail to hit pay dirt."

"I'll fetch the Rover. It can't be more than one kilometer distant."

With little over an hour of daylight remaining, the two miners commenced shoveling away the drifted sand, thankful for the low Martian gravity. In the span of forty minutes they had succeeded in removing a considerable amount of lightly packed sand. While the end of one extra long pair of grooves still lay buried, the two converging gouges had very nearly come together to form a point.

"How much further?" Chadwick asked, beginning to weary from the task.

"Until darkness or treasure, whichever comes first," replied his companion, refusing to admit that he was also tiring.

A few minutes later they were rewarded by a sudden glimpse of something metallic beneath the rust colored sand. Continuing to dig, it was not long before they stood gazing upon an incredible scene.

"Christ! What in heaven's name is that?" shouted Chadwick, over their radio link.

"An archeological find of cosmic proportions, I should say," replied Thompson, digging with renewed vigor.

The two excited explorers continued to excavate until darkness threatened to overtake them. Whatever it was they had discovered, further investigation would have to wait until morning. Exhausted by their efforts, they stood in awe at what they had uncovered: a silvery metallic door that was built into the side of the cliff face - *unmistakable proof that an alien civilization had once inhabited the planet Mars!*

Chapter 4

THE ROSETTA STONE

Forced to retire to the protective environment of the Rover, the two astronauts found it difficult to contain their excitement. Eventually establishing contact with the orbiting Mars Voyager, they hastened to transmit video pictures of their incredible find. One could well imagine the great fervor and descriptive newspaper headlines back on Earth. It was unquestionably the most profound single event in the history of mankind!

Neither Chadwick nor Thompson felt the need for sleep that night, although their aching muscles were grateful for the rest. When they did awaken at dawn, from a rather sporadic and limited slumber, it was to a cabin temperature just a few degrees above freezing. Regrettably, their dwindling reserve of electrical power had dictated a very low thermostat setting.

"It's times like this which makes me think of warm tropical beaches," chattered the shivering geologist.

"Do you think we'll be able to open this mysterious door?" asked Thompson, more concerned with thoughts of discovery than with the mundane issue of enduring a slight chill.

"There has to be a way in. Nobody's going to construct a door that won't open."

"But we don't have a key and we forgot to bring along burglar tools," remarked Thompson.

"I sure hope we don't have to come back with a locksmith. We had enough trouble getting here the first time."

"If we can't gain entry any discoveries will have to await another expedition from Earth. We have neither explosives nor a cutting torch," Thompson pointed out.

"Well, we'll soon know," said Chadwick. "It shouldn't take us long to clear away the rest of the drifted sand."

"I would say less than an hour. We've already dug down to the original ground level at one end of the door."

"Then let's eat and get on with it. All this talk of digging is giving me an appetite."

With the outside temperature still well below zero, the two adventurers exited the Rover's air lock and eagerly set about removing the balance of the sand which concealed a mysterious door to whatever lay beyond. Barely twenty minutes into the task they made a significant discovery.

"I think I've found it!" exclaimed Thompson.

"What have you uncovered?" asked his colleague, coming over to investigate.

"It appears to be some sort of lever," stated Thompson, upon examining a protrusion on the face of the otherwise smooth surface of the door. "I can only assume that its function is to afford access."

"Let's finish excavating the rest of this sand before we try our luck with it," suggested Chadwick.

In a matter of minutes they stood looking at a fully exposed door, measuring approximately three meters high by four meters wide. The protruding lever was situated less than one meter from the left-hand side of the door, a little over a meter above ground level. It extended horizontally, and was accompanied by eroded markings on the door in the form of converging grooved arcs which began just below the open end of the lever.

"Unless I miss my guess, I have to interpret these markings as an instruction to pull down on the lever," Thompson deduced.

"Seems plausible to me," agreed Chadwick. "Let's go for it."

Grasping the lever, Thompson pulled down. It moved slowly but smoothly, offering moderate resistance. Upon reaching a vertical position it simply refused to go any further. The door, however, remained closed.

"It would seem that our cosmic builders neglected to install an automatic garage door opener," quipped Chadwick.

"Maybe they failed to pay their electric bill," Thompson was quick to suggest. "Think we should knock?"

"Perhaps a good kick would be more effective."

"Why don't we try pushing? If this mechanism is as old as I suspect it's bound to be a trifle rusty," said Thompson, giving the door a firm shove.

Nothing happened.

"Let's try together, on the count of three," suggested the geologist.

"Agreed."

"One....two....three....push!" shouted Chadwick.

They pushed. Again, nothing happened.

"I thought I felt a slight movement," declared Thompson. "Let's take a run at it and hit it with our shoulders."

"I'm game, but if this doesn't work the first time you can count me out for a repeat performance. I've always disliked running into brick walls."

Backing up some distance, they charged the stubborn door together and struck it with considerable force - their momentum sending them sprawling into the abyss of a dark and mysterious chamber, as the door suddenly swung open.

From a prone position on the chamber floor the two intruders eventually concluded that the only damage was to their dignity. Regrettably, with the limited amount of sunlight filtering in through the partially open door, they could see very little.

"Nobody ever told me that exploring could be so degrading," remarked Chadwick, picking himself up and shaking off some dust.

"I suspect these minor irritations are some deity's way of testing us," philosophized Thompson, as he prepared to address the lighting problem.

Unfortunately, even with the door wide open they could view only a short distance inside. What they could see clearly, in the unpressurized chamber, was the floor. It appeared to consist of a non-slip glassy substance. As near as they could determine, the walls seemed to be of similar composition. Artificial lighting of some sort was essential, however, if they were to examine the far reaches of the chamber.

"About the only option we have before us is to bring in the Rover and turn on the headlights," Thompson concluded.

"Just what we needed to run down our storage batteries. But you're right, of course, we've come too far not to know what's at the other end of this alien structure," reasoned Chadwick.

"I'll get the Rover," said Thompson, moving toward the open doorway. "Try not to get into any mischief while I'm gone."

"Don't worry, I won't go far. I can't see a damn thing beyond the immediate entrance."

In a short while Thompson returned with the Rover. Driving it through the doorway he turned on the dual headlights, illuminating the interior and revealing a puzzling scene. Smack in the middle of the spacious chamber was a solitary object: a glistening silver cylinder! No other material structure was visible, although a number of markings and images could be seen etched on the walls and ceiling. Also, a bright green door could be observed at the far end of the elongated chamber, which was subsequently found to measure roughly twelve by seventy meters, with an arched ceiling estimated to range from four meters to at least ten meters.

The door drew their immediate attention. What treasures or secrets lay beyond? Rectangular in shape, it was of substantial size, measuring almost three meters wide by just over two meters high. A series of control buttons could be seen, arranged in a circular pattern. Each was inscribed with a different symbol. There was no lever or doorknob visible.

"It has to be the entrance to an air lock," ventured Thompson, as he examined the metallic barrier at close hand.

"I would have to agree," said Chadwick. "It's inconceivable that the aliens could live in the thin carbon dioxide atmosphere of this planet."

"Which of these buttons do we activate in order to enter?" asked Thompson, staring at the meaningless inscriptions imprinted on the array of push buttons.

"Or which combination?" added Chadwick.

"I've always liked to experiment," said Thompson, pushing one button after another until all seven buttons had been tried.

Nothing happened.

"Care to have a go at it?" asked Thompson, following a number of unsuccessful attempts. "I seem to have struck out."

Having no better luck, Chadwick was also forced to concede defeat, finally giving the door a vigorous push and then a solid kick - all to no avail.

"I don't suppose you want to try the running charge attack, again?" quipped Thompson. "I could put down the video camera and assist you."

"Forget it! One humiliation per day is enough."

"It will evidently necessitate a future expedition armed with a cutting torch - unless some deity gives us the combination," remarked Thompson.

"Either that, or a good safecracker."

After video taping a close-up view of the green door, with its enigmatic push button symbols, they focused attention upon the equally mysterious silver capsule.

"What do you suppose the cylinder contains?" asked Chadwick, as the two approached the alien artifact.

"Beats me! But whatever it is must be of some importance. Otherwise, why would it be placed in the exact center of the chamber?"

They bent over to examine the capsule in greater detail. Well over one meter in diameter, it was about three meters in length. While somewhat truncated, the two ends were rounded to form a dull point. Adorning the top was what resembled four handles, two at each end. A series of converging grooves drew attention to what appeared to be a solitary push button, situated at one end of the cylinder.

"Are we to presume that this button affords the key to gaining access?" hypothesized Thompson.

"Sounds like a viable theory to me," agreed Chadwick. "Short of cutting it open, I don't see any other way in."

"Well, here goes," said Thompson, giving the button a sharp jab with his finger.

As they watched, the nearby end of the cylinder swung open, revealing an interior which resembled a highly elongated filing cabinet. Row upon row of (plastic/metal?) sheets, each about 3 mm thick, could be seen resting upon a rolling track mechanism.

"It could very well be a repository for alien knowledge," said Thompson, grasping hold of a convenient handle and giving it a gentle pull.

The contents of the capsule slid toward him, disclosing an estimated one thousand "data sheets." Cursory examination showed that they were arranged in a definite order. The sheets at the front consisted entirely of pictures with a simple accompanying logo; while the later ones contained a preponderance of somewhat more elaborate symbols and complex text.

"What do you make of it?" Chadwick asked.

"Offhand, I would have to say that it conveys a record of the alien civilization. But it also looks as if it might possess a built-in *Rosetta Stone* dictionary!" exclaimed Thompson, scarcely able to contain his excitement.

"You mean that the aliens have deliberately chosen to give us insight into their language?" responded Chadwick.

"That's exactly what I mean. It positively boggles the mind just to think of what we could learn."

"But where are they? What happened to them? Are they lurking behind the closed green door?" Chadwick wanted to know.

"Perhaps these records will tell us, once we manage to decode them. Unquestionably, it becomes of paramount importance to bring this capsule back to Earth."

"I certainly agree....Say, just how heavy do you think it is?" Chadwick asked, by way of an afterthought.

"Let's find out," said Thompson, pushing the contents back into the cylinder and closing the lid.

"Seems to be a simple catch mechanism," remarked Chadwick, as he checked the lid to make sure that it was fastened securely.

Together, they grasped handles at opposite ends of the capsule and began to lift. To their considerable relief, weight would not present a difficulty in the low Martian gravity. It was nothing that the two astronauts could not manage.

"My guess would be about one hundred kilograms if measured in terms of Earth gravity," announced Thompson, taking steps toward the Rover.

As anticipated, it was too long to allow them to close the rear door of the vehicle's unpressurized storage compartment. A protrusion in excess of one meter could not be avoided. All other dimensions would not pose a problem.

"Better put the push button end in first," suggested Thompson. "That way, if the lid should jar loose, at least the contents of our prize would not spill out over the Martian countryside."

"Affirmative," acknowledged the geologist, as they proceeded to slide the alien artifact into the back of the Rover.

Using the versatile climbing rope to secure their trophy in the vehicle's cargo bay, they felt confident that it would suffice for the return trip to the Explorer. With another length of cord they managed to tie down the open hatch.

"Never visit a strange planet without rope," said Thompson, giving the overhanging cylinder a vigorous tug by way of a final test. "I don't know what we would have done without it."

"Believe it or not, but it was all I could do to convince one official of this very need," Chadwick confessed. "Although I must admit that I was thinking only in terms of ascending our peculiar rock."

"Well, in that case, you should be able to gloat over your fortuitous foresight," commented Thompson, turning to look at images and symbols inscribed on a nearby wall.

"The lighting is lousy," complained Chadwick. "I doubt if I could read it even if I understood the language."

"Why don't we scan with the video camera on CCD mode? When the images are computer enhanced they should give satisfactory resolution."

"Let's do it."

During the course of the next ten minutes they meticulously scanned all four walls, along with the arched ceiling. In a few places the light was sufficient to reveal a limited amount of detail. One scene appeared to be that of a seascape; while a second showed a group of hominoid figures in front of a strange looking machine. Other images portrayed exotic and unfamiliar forms of vegetation. But the one image which really caught their eye was that of an aerial view of the mysterious Martian "Face." Extending the full height of the wall, it was clearly discernible, even in the poor and unequal illumination of the Rover's dual headlights.

"They evidently thought enough of their impressive sculptoring project as to enshrine a picture of it as a wall mural," Thompson remarked.

"There's just no way that I can believe the vegetation and seascape are indigenous to this planet," voiced Chadwick.

"It's my opinion that the builders of this structure are not native Martians," stated Thompson. "They must have come from another solar system, heaven only knows how many centuries ago."

"There certainly doesn't seem to be anybody around here now."

"Want to give one last kick on their door before we depart?"

asked Thompson.

"Feel free to leave them a note, if you desire. I expect it will produce the same result."

Still pondering the fate of the alien civilization, the two amateur archeologists prepared to terminate exploration of what was merely an outer chamber - beyond which undoubtedly lay a vast labyrinth of other rooms and other treasures.

"It's frustrating that we couldn't gain access," lamented the geologist, as they approached the Rover.

"I only hope that I get to participate in a return mission," remarked Thompson.

"Ditto," echoed his companion.

"Say, it might be best if I cycle through the air lock alone. Someone should close the garage door after I exit with the Rover," Thompson suggested.

"Good idea. A great deal of sand and dust could blow inside before mankind is likely to return. It might take forever to vacuum it all out."

With the door resealed, it was exactly one hour before Martian high noon as the two adventurers began the long trek back to the Explorer. In a short while the Mars Voyager would be in position to establish contact. They could hardly wait to convey essentials of the startling news. It was not every day that Earth society would find irrefutable evidence of an alien civilization from a planet belonging to another solar system!

"At least the trip back should be easy navigation, as we have only to retrace our path," said Thompson. "In fact, many of our tracks are clearly visible."

"It should also take less time," Chadwick added. "We won't have to experiment with blind alleys strewn with boulders."

"On the other hand, there is a possibility that we might have to get out and walk the last few kilometers. That episode with the Rover's headlights was a totally unforeseen battery-draining experience," reminded Thompson.

"I see what you mean. With the fuel cell depleted, and our batteries at considerably less than half charge, we could have a problem."

"It could well be a photo finish."

"It's very likely to be worse than that," Chadwick finally announced, glancing at figures appearing on a computer screen. "Even with the solar panels at full efficiency, I still come up with a deficit."

"How much of a deficit?"

"Somewhere between 10 to 15 kilometers."

"Any chance of finding us a shorter route?" asked Thompson, not really expecting other than a negative reply.

"I wouldn't advise it. You know what happened when we tried to go between those two craters."

"Don't remind me."

"I'm afraid we'll just have to resign ourselves to becoming pedestrians, at some point in our homeward trek," sighed Chadwick.

"Cheer up! Things could be worse," Thompson philosophized. "At least it's not the season for sand storms."

Further conversation was cut short by a loud buzzing sound and a flashing yellow light on the vehicle's control panel.

"It's the Mars Voyager attempting to contact us," said the geologist, flipping a switch which would open an audio channel.

The adventurers wasted no time in describing their remarkable find inside the "Face." They were also quick to stress the need for a second expedition to discover what lay beyond the enigmatic locked door. Unable to communicate directly with the Explorer, they requested that an update of information be forwarded at once - including the prediction that the Rover would likely run out of electrical power some distance short of their destination.

"Tell them to send out a search party if we don't make it," said Chadwick.

"No matter what, the alien capsule must be recovered and sent back to Earth for detailed analysis," Thompson hastened to add, before signing off.

"Will do," acknowledged Yamoto, aboard the orbiting mother ship.

"I'll make it clear to Brodsky that he better not come back without you guys," said Maladev.

"We'll be sure to pass on your latest coordinates every time we can get a fix on your position," promised Yamoto.

Hour after hour the Rover plodded across the bleak Martian landscape. Their outgoing tracks made it possible for them to travel at a higher rate of speed, since they no longer had to be so wary of every rock or crevasse which might spell disaster.

"At least we don't have to watch out for oncoming traffic," remarked Thompson, as they approached the midway point of their journey.

"I only wish there was some traffic," responded his companion. "It's sure going to be difficult hitching a ride out here."

"What's the update on our power reserves versus distance to be covered?" Thompson inquired.

"Less than 17% battery. It still comes out as a deficit of 10 to 15 kilometers, and that's assuming no unforeseen drain."

"I can't think of any way to reduce consumption. We haven't used any juice for cabin heating since a very limited amount last night," said Thompson.

"Yeah, and we damn near froze to death!"

"Didn't I recommend a heavier sweater?"

"You know, Adam, it's too bad we couldn't have stashed extra batteries at some intermediate point on our route. Even another fuel cell would have come in handy."

"That's what comes from not getting your priorities right," said Thompson. "Nobody at Mission Control ever took this trip seriously. If anything, it was just an afterthought to appease a highly imaginative public."

"How true!"

"You can bet that when we return, some years hence, every effort will be made to land as close as possible to the alien structure," remarked Thompson.

A few hours later the inevitable occurred. The Rover, its batteries exhausted, coasted to a dead stop. With no possibility of recharging them, it would have to be abandoned. According to Chadwick's estimate, they were approximately 12 km away from the Explorer. Their last contact with the Mars Voyager had been about an hour ago, when they were still more than 40 km away from their destination.

"Well, I guess this means we'll have to hoof it from here," said Thompson, unfastening his seat belt.

"We have over three hours of daylight remaining," advised the geologist/navigator.

"Plenty of time to cover the distance on foot," said Thompson. "As long as our outgoing tracks are visible we won't have to worry about getting lost."

"I certainly don't fancy staying here overnight. It could get rather chilly without heat," commented Chadwick.

"It's unfortunate that we can't establish communication with the Explorer," remarked Thompson.

"We have a sizable impact crater and a number of hills between us which are blocking transmission," said Chadwick, following yet another futile attempt to raise their landing craft.

"I can't see waiting around to contact the Mars Voyager again. Our last estimate of power depletion was quite accurate, and it's doubtful if our location could be pinpointed any better," Thompson reasoned.

"I agree," said Chadwick. "They've already been informed that we plan to depart immediately, on foot, once our batteries have gone flat."

"You know, Martin, I believe we could take the alien capsule with us, rather than leave it here for a rescue party."

"Don't you think that's asking a lot? That cylinder isn't exactly weightless."

"Have you forgotten the rope?"

"You mean," said Chadwick, "that we could pull it?"

"Precisely!"

"Seems logical. I suppose if it becomes too tiring we could always leave the capsule and retrieve it in the morning."

"We should have no trouble finding it, and it would save us retracing a great many steps."

"Let's do it," said Chadwick, as he rose from his seat and prepared to don a space suit.

"First, however, I'm going to leave behind a taped message stating our plans," Thompson declared. "I'll simply program the computer to relay it to the Mars Voyager when they next attempt to establish contact."

Some twenty minutes later the two explorers had removed the alien artifact from the Rover and were ready to begin their 12 km trek. With the rope fashioned into a makeshift harness, they were pleased to find that the capsule slid quite nicely across the sand of the Martian surface. Assisted by the relatively low gravity of the planet, it was not as difficult as it would have been back on Earth.

"I'm sure glad that we have our old tracks to follow," said Thompson. "Without a compass, as we are, it would be so easy to become disoriented."

"I agree. Even though we brought our map with us a lot of these craters and rolling hills tend to look alike."

"We seem to be making good progress."

"Indeed we are," responded Chadwick. "I doubt if the cylinder is holding us back by more than one or two kilometers per hour."

"At this rate we should be home in time for dinner."

"I can't wait to see their faces when we show them the video tapes we took," said the geologist.

"Especially the scene where you gave the green door a swift kick," chuckled Thompson.

"What? You taped that caper?"

"It was one of the highlights of the whole trip."

"I guess it was kind of funny at that."

In joyful spirits, they passed over the crest of a hill and started down a moderately steep slope. All at once their carefree composure changed to one of concern. Of their outgoing tracks there was not a trace! Only a barren windswept surface, composed of rock and ancient lava deposits, was visible.

"Christ!" exclaimed Chadwick. "The wind must have stripped away the thin layer of sand and dust."

With the Rover's tracks effectively obliterated, they came to an abrupt halt and pondered the situation. They had covered an estimated four kilometers, with another eight to go. The last thing they wanted to do was to get lost.

"To pursue our present heading we should probably make for a point midway between the small impact crater on our right and the distant ridge over there," said Thompson, pointing with his gloved finger. "How does such reasoning compare with the map?"

"Appears to jibe. Let's hope we can find tracks on the next series of hills."

Resuming a brisk walking pace they set off again. With less than two hours of daylight left they could not afford to waste a moment.

Nor could they afford to get disoriented. Even if their limited supply of oxygen held out the bitterly cold Martian night posed a deadly threat.

"Still no sign of any tracks," remarked Thompson, as they came to the crest of yet another hill.

"Damn! I was expecting to pick up the trail by now. There's a cluster of small craters directly ahead. Which side do we go around?" Thompson asked, calling a momentary halt so his companion could once more consult their map.

"If we bypass to the left we should come to a plain scattered with boulders. The Explorer should be just over a line of high hills, about two or three kilometers beyond."

"O.K. Let's go," said Thompson. "Time is of the essence."

Passing the craters, they soon gazed upon a horizon replete with multiple hills - all of which looked very much the same! Lacking a compass they had only the position of the Sun, now quite low in the sky, to guide them. They made a turn of some thirty degrees, hoping that their sense of direction had not failed them.

"Which valley do we head for?" asked Thompson. "We seem to have a choice."

"Your guess is as good as mine," said Chadwick.

"You make the decision," responded Thompson. "If you're wrong I can always blame you for getting us lost."

"Oh, great!"

"Don't worry, if your advice proves good I promise to be the first to praise your keen sense of navigation."

They plodded on, cursing the many times they had to detour around massive rocks and boulders. A scattering of tiny impact craters contributed to their annoyance. There was still no trace of any outbound tracks as they finally emerged from the obstacle maze and entered a small valley between two steep hills. Upon passing through, they came to a large plain with gentle rolling hills, any one of which could conceal a spaceship. There was no sign of the Explorer! To make matters worse, the Sun was on the verge of setting.

"I think our best bet is for one of us to climb a hill," said Thompson. "Unless we're really off course it should be possible to spot the Explorer."

"Excellent idea," agreed Chadwick. "I'll volunteer. As you may recall, I'm supposed to be the climbing expert."

Reaching into a pocket of his space suit, Thompson extracted a pair of diminutive flashlights. Clipping one to his utility belt, he gave the other to his companion. "There's very little twilight in this thin atmosphere," he said. "Small as they are, they will be our only means of finding each other in the dark."

"I'll try the hill on our left," said Chadwick. "It looks as if it might be the easiest one to climb."

"Good hunting," said Thompson, as his fellow explorer set off at a trot for the hill, estimated to be about 200 meters high.

"I think I should be able to reach the top before we lose all light," voiced Chadwick, over his radio link.

"Acknowledged," said Thompson. "See if you can raise our colleagues once you get there."

"Will do."

One hundred meters from the summit Chadwick paused and began to scan the landscape. No spacecraft was visible. However, he could presently view only a portion of the terrain suspected of harboring the Explorer. He moved higher and to his left in order to rectify the situation. To his dismay, the Sun had just set. "Can you still hear me, Adam?" he asked.

"Barely," came the weak reply.

"Speak louder!" came a request that did not sound at all like Thompson.

"Brodsky, is that you?" asked Chadwick.

"Affirmative! But where are you?"

"On top of a hill. Where are you?"

"Also on top of a hill. Where's Adam?"

"Adam is waiting below with our alien treasure."

"We can only hear you. Can you see our light?"

At last, reaching a more favorable position, Chadwick looked down at the silhouette of the Explorer's upper stage, its lights shining distinctly about two kilometers away. He could also see a light on a neighboring hilltop. He pointed his small flashlight in the direction of Brodsky's light.

"We can see your light," came Jeffery Walker's voice over his helmet radio.

"I've just spotted the Explorer," said Chadwick. "We should be able to make it back within the hour. Don't eat without us."

Retracing his steps down the hillside in the dark was more difficult than climbing it in daylight. Twice Chadwick fell, but managed to pick himself up with no apparent harm. He could see Thompson's light in the distance. Without it he could have found himself wandering aimlessly around in search of his companion.

"I told them to expect us for dinner," said the geologist, as the two adventurers were finally united at the base of what would henceforth be known as Chadwick Hill.

"How far away are we?"

"About two kilometers. We need to make a 45 degree turn to the left after we pass our historic hill."

"Then let's go!" exclaimed Thompson, setting himself in the rope harness. "I'm starting to get hungry."

Trudging across the Martian landscape in almost total darkness was far from a picnic. The meager illumination provided by their flashlights did not prevent them from stumbling a number of times. Directly above them the largest and innermost moon, Phobos, cast a feeble but welcome glow over the bleak surface. Appearing about one-third as large as Earth's satellite, it moved from west to east, the opposite of normal planetary moons. Deimos, looking like a bright star, was visible just above the eastern horizon.

With only one kilometer to go they were joined by Brodsky and Walker. Together, the four astronauts continued at a steady pace toward the Explorer, its lights now clearly visible ahead of them. With the temperature already well below zero, they could feel the chill in their bones and began to entertain thoughts of a hot meal and warm surroundings.

"Sorry we caused you fellows so much trouble," said Chadwick, content to let Walker and Brodsky have a go at pulling the alien capsule.

"You know, it's a great shame that we were forced to abandon the Rover," remarked Thompson. "Unfortunately, we were unable to find an electric filling station."

"Not to worry," said Brodsky. "We were planning to dump it in a few days anyhow."

"The artifact you brought back is priceless. Whether you two realize it or not you're classified as heroes back home on Earth," Walker informed them.

"Does this mean we get a raise?" quipped Chadwick, as the open hatch of the Explorer loomed before their eyes.

"Let's drop our treasure here," suggested Brodsky. "We can load it aboard tomorrow in daylight."

"Sounds like a good idea," agreed Thompson. "I doubt if any burglar is going to swipe it."

"I'm told that Chou Lin has prepared a huge feast by way of a celebration," stated Walker.

"Last one up the ladder has to wash dishes," said Chadwick, as he made a dash for the cargo bay ramp.

....

As dawn gave way to early morning, the astronauts faced the task of lifting their archeological treasure up to the pressurized crew compartment. A problem of sorts was posed by the dimensions of the alien artifact. Even if it would fit into the air lock, its considerable length forbid passage around the exhaust nozzle of the ascent engine. While a man could very easily effect this detour, the rigid structure of the metallic cylinder precluded such contortion. In short, it became obvious that the contents of the capsule would have to be removed and taken aboard piecemeal.

After pondering the matter at length, a plan of action was devised. Utilizing blankets and sleeping bags as receptacles, they would tie together bundles of the plastic/metal sheets and haul them up the four stories of the central passageway. While the protective cylinder would have to be left behind, its truly precious contents could be transported intact to Earth. So as to preserve the order of the "data sheets," which was thought by all to constitute pages of an informative Celestial Book - complete with a *"Rosetta Stone"* dictionary - it was agreed that great care must be taken not to mix them out of context.

"Rope to the rescue again!" exclaimed Thompson, as he began pulling the first bundle toward the upper stage air lock.

"I'm sure it will be made standard issue for all future space missions," responded Chadwick, who was standing on a platform at the top of the descent module.

"How many loads will there be?" asked Thompson, through the radio link of his suit.

"Brodsky says he has made a total of seven packages, carefully labeled and in proper sequence."

"I can hardly wait to have a more detailed look at the alien pictures and symbols," said Thompson. "I have a feeling that my good friend, Professor Matt Duncan, would just love to get his hands on them."

Four hours later, with their treasure safely loaded, the five astronauts aboard the Explorer prepared to lift off and rendezvous with their orbiting mother ship. Having accomplished all major objectives, and without the mobility afforded by the Rover, there was now little point in delaying departure. A convenient launch window was fast approaching and the countdown was in progress.

"Ignition!" shouted Brodsky, flipping a switch.

A tongue of orange flame shot from the nozzle of the ascent stage and spewed through the open hatch of the descent module. With rapidly increasing speed the craft rose through the tenuous Martian atmosphere. Some ten minutes later they were tracking the Mars Voyager on their radar screen.

"Thirty-four minutes to intercept," said Thompson.

"Trajectory and rate of closure right on the mark," announced Yamoto, from the mother ship. "We look forward to welcoming you guys back."

Docking of the two spacecraft proceeded without incident, and it was not long before both parties were united. Exchanging a profusion of greetings, they wasted little time in transferring their precious cargo. It seemed a shame to abandon what was left of the Explorer, but it was simply not feasible to expend the fuel needed to return it to Earth. Having served its purpose well, it was with a measure of sadness that they cast it loose.

A few orbits later they began the return trip. Igniting a series of solid fuel rockets, the Mars Voyager broke free of the Red Planet's gravitational hold and commenced a long spiral path toward a distant blue/white globe called home.

Chapter 5

REVELATION

The lush green vegetation of Professor Duncan's semi-tropical garden was in marked contrast to a bleak Martian landscape. Likewise, the deep blue sky overhead was more colorful and pleasing to the eye than the inky blackness of space, permeated only by tiny points of light, now projected on the large TV screen before an audience of five attentive viewers. Seated on the patio beside the professor was his fiancee, Erica Williams. Also present were Janet Thompson and the twins, Susan and Robert. They were drawn together to watch the triumphant return of the Mars Voyager, after its historic journey of discovery to the Red Planet.

The video picture changed to reveal a most spectacular view of Space Station Prometheus, taken from a nearby shuttle craft. In a short while it would record the actual docking itself. For the moment, however, the telephoto lense of its camera could only pick up a small and quite unresolvable image, which was declared by the announcer to be the famous spacecraft. Currently some hundreds of kilometers away, it was not expected to dock for at least another twenty minutes. At this point the TV scene abruptly reverted to a commercial advertising a specific brand of breakfast cereal.

"Say, Matt, didn't you promise to tell us more about your new cosmological theories?" asked Janet. "My children have bugged me to remind you of your commitment."

"Yes, please do," said Erica. "A promise is a promise, even after ten months."

"You people sure have good memories," replied the professor.

"I believe you were going to discuss quasars and the issue of creation," said Robert.

Professor Duncan endeavored to elucidate as follows:

"As I recall, it was suggested that matter is probably created in the form of infinitesimal quanta - presumably, many billions of times smaller than the electron. I would also infer that creation involves equal numbers of oppositely rotating entities. Moreover, it is assumed that this rotation is responsible for the electrical charge exhibited by matter. (Although it might be wondered how opposite rotation could be preserved when such corpuscles might approach each other at any one of innumerable angles, this problem is removed simply by ascribing both polar and equatorial rotation. No matter how such spherical bodies are brought together, their surfaces will continue to express the same flow characteristics of harmony or disharmony wherever they touch.)

"In order for these elementary forms to evolve into mature physical particles, such as electrons and protons, it is necessary to appeal to the repulsive nature of gravitation. With this force acting to compress newly created quanta, toward a central point between surrounding superclusters of galaxies, a relatively small region of very high density is eventually produced - essentially, a massive rotating black hole, which continues to grow and to completely dominate the structure of nearby mass/energy.

"As these infinitesimal quanta spiral toward each other they are induced to undergo fusion into fewer entities of greater value. The question now arises as to what terminates evolution and produces stable particles. In essence, the explanation must be found in a fundamental law of physics requiring an increase of rotation with an increase of mass. Accordingly, once a critical degree of rotation is achieved, it will serve to prohibit the incorporation of additional quanta. Such a stage is reached at the electron/positron level. From this point on the evolution of matter must proceed through fusion of quantities of electrons and positrons. Again, the principle of rapid rotation must provide the mechanism which terminates fusion at the proton level. The mystery of why protons are not accompanied by an equal number of antiprotons is likely due to the rotary direction of the black hole creation zone, as fusion of electrons and positrons must be precluded in any direction contrary to the prevailing flow.

"The temporary existence of a free neutron requires a more subtle explanation. Produced in the high temperature and density of stellar interiors, a neutron may be described as a proton with an electron nucleus jammed inside its halo of orbiting quanta - requiring only a chance encounter with an exceptionally massive quantum to permit escape from the system. Within atomic nuclei the neutrons are able to hold together protons, which would tend to repel each other by reason of their like charges. (Unlike charges attract; while like charges repel.) Protons do this by exchanging a nuclear electron, so that at any given instant one of the protons may be considered to be a neutron. This ability of an electron to neutralize a proton's charge is duplicated in the swirling energy of an atom's halo, where it is able to disrupt or cancel the rotary flow of associated quanta.

"To return to the phenomenon of a rapidly rotating black hole creation site, it may well be asked how vast quantities of newly created hydrogen came to be distributed throughout the depths of space. Invariably, the answer must be attributed to the extreme rotation of the black hole centered creation zone. Initially prevented from expelling matter by the sheer volume of inflowing quanta, it is merely a question of time until the rotary force increases to the point where it becomes the dominant factor. Once this stage is reached it must result in a mammoth explosion, in which the vast bulk of evolving matter forms are blasted deep into space - from whence this hydrogen (and some primordial helium) gas is permitted by gravitation to condense into a new generation of stars and galaxies.

"Such a *Small Bang* explosion is not likely to be so readily observed as a supernova, since the former is characterized by a gravitational field many trillions of times greater, which acts to effectively mask any outward flow of radiation. What is left is a supermassive black hole surrounded by enough orbital matter as to constitute a quasar which, in time, evolves into a very massive galaxy. Within our own supercluster, the giant M87 galaxy was probably still recognizable as a quasar a dozen billion years ago.

"Inasmuch as the luminosity of a quasar is an indication of age, in the sense that the younger the brighter, it may be adduced that this knowledge must have profound cosmological implications. If the concept of annihilation at the cosmic edge is valid, it is to be inferred that a preponderance of high luminosity quasars is to be found in the direction of the nearby edge, since many of them will not have had sufficient time to age and grow feeble. This has indeed proven to be the case, affording strong evidence that we are presently situated in an extremely eccentric location. It also confirms my assumption, based upon quasar distribution, in which an exceptionally high number are revealed to populate the nearby edge in the vicinity of the constellation of Sculptor."

"Have you been able to determine exactly how close we are to this fateful boundary of the universe?" asked Janet.

"Not yet," replied Professor Duncan. "But there are certain clues which may prove useful in resolving this issue."

"And what may they be?" Janet wanted to know.

"One method involves a study of discordant redshifts," said the professor. "Ever since the latter half of the 20th century, astronomers have noted instances where gravitationally entwined galaxies exhibit very different redshifts. Moreover, some of these discrepancies are so great as to imply separations of a hundred million light-years or more! I now have good reason to suspect that all of these anomalies are related to the manner in which inbound radiation is virtually trapped in close proximity to the cosmic edge."

"You mean that a small separation between galaxies, in direct line of sight toward the nearby cosmic boundary, acts to greatly magnify radiation transit times?" responded Janet.

"Precisely!" remarked the professor, delighted that his star pupil was able to follow his reasoning. "According to studies that I have recently made, all of these discordant redshifts may be reduced to plausible levels if it were to be conceded that we currently reside within just a few million light-years from the cosmic periphery. In fact, there is a possibility that it could be somewhat less."

"Good heavens!" exclaimed Janet. "How much less?"

"At this moment I honestly don't know," answered Professor Duncan. "But there is another way to reduce present uncertainty. Shortly after the discordant redshift issue arose, it was reported that the redshifts of many members of our Local Supercluster are actually declining with the passage of time - evidently, by as much as 1-2 km per second per decade! If I could determine the difference in speed of propagation - between radiation and the D/R (distance/repulsion) aspect of gravitation - it should be possible to calculate our proximity to the cosmic edge, as it is a factor very much related to the rate of any decline of redshift."

"I'm afraid you have me there, Matt," confessed Janet.

"I can conceive of only one way in which this strange decline may be explained - a decline which must surely be a comparatively recent development," said the professor. "Since a large component of galactic redshifts is nonvelocity in nature - being caused by increased transit time due to encounters with concentrations of D/R quanta - it is to be inferred that this mysterious reduction is the result of a changing flow of such quanta. As there is good reason to suspect that gravitation propagates slightly faster than radiation, the last of an extinct galaxy's D/R quanta will have passed us while its radiation is still in transit. In effect, our Milky Way will suddenly be deprived of the D/R quanta needed to slow incoming radiation - producing a sharp decline in redshifts of many members of our supercluster!"

"Why do you think gravitation is able to propagate faster than radiation?" asked Robert, disproving any notion that the subject was beyond his comprehension.

"The very premise that gravitation flows freely from a black hole, whereas radiation cannot, is a clear indication that this must be so," answered the professor.

Further conversation was cut short as the TV screen began to convey a remarkable series of images. No longer a tiny point of light, the Mars Voyager could now be seen in considerable detail. Lacking the great cluster of solid fuel rockets with which it had departed, it appeared much slimmer and more like a science fiction spacecraft. Gone also was the large appendage in the form of the Explorer. Such an expenditure was clearly a small price to pay for what promised to be knowledge beyond mankind's wildest dreams.

They watched in silence as the historic ship slowly maneuvered to a docking position at the hub of Prometheus. Utilizing the air lock which once provided access to the Explorer, a seal was soon established with its protruding counterpart on the orbiting space station. The television scene promptly shifted to the interior of Prometheus, where a host of dignitaries and reporters awaited the returning heroes.

In a gesture of appreciation, it had been decided that the two co-discoverers of the alien civilization would be accorded first right of entry and conversation with the news media. After what seemed an eternity the door finally opened.

"Look! There's daddy!" shouted Susan, as Adam Thompson and

Martin Chadwick made their appearance, waving together to a TV audience estimated to exceed four billion viewers.

Robert was positively beaming as the duo were praised for their outstanding achievement. Tears of joy could be detected rolling down Janet's pretty face.

"How long will it be before my father is allowed to return to Earth?" Robert wanted to know.

"Unless there is an unforeseen change of plans it should be another three days," responded Erica. "The crew will be debriefed and given a complete physical examination before departing on one of the two shuttles currently docked at the space station."

"I wonder if the alien's data sheets will give us insight into their cosmology?" remarked Erica.

"I certainly hope so," said Professor Duncan. "I very much look forward to the task of decoding them."

....

During the span of the next seven months significant progress was made in interpreting the alien symbols. As anticipated, an International Team, which included the world's most renowned and talented linguists, was assembled to decode the enigmatic text. Also, as Professor Duncan had hoped, he was asked to be a member of the team. In fact, largely through the insistence of his good friend, Thompson, he was made chairman of this privileged group.

Just as Thompson had surmised, the initial section of the data sheets was in the form of a *"Rosetta Stone"* dictionary, designed to afford insight into the alien's language. Although a great deal remained to be understood, it was felt that the Team had now acquired a reasonably adequate grasp of what were acknowledged to be totally foreign symbols. Assisted by the use of sophisticated computers, the group had succeeded in deriving a most informative picture of a society that had once lived on Mars.

According to the alien records the builders of the "Face" were not indigenous to the Red Planet, as had long been suspected by virtually all Earth scientists. Instead, they came from another planet and another solar system. Their distant home world was called "Selestia," and it was also the third planet from a "G" type star not too dissimilar to our Sun. Its distance was thought to be of the order of 70 light-years. The Selestians were clearly an older and more advanced race, having attained space capability an estimated 30,000 Earth years prior to their departure for our Solar System.

A number of pressing questions immediately came to mind. Why did the Selestians ever leave their planet, on a lengthy voyage that must have extended over many generations? Why settle on an essentially barren planet, when Earth was just a small step away? Had they, in fact, ever visited Earth? How long did they stay? Where were they now? Why did they construct the "Face" on Mars? When did they create this amazing structure? As it turned out, answers to these questions were to be found in the alien data sheets.

Having reached an advanced stage of development, in which interstellar travel no longer posed a problem, the Selestians considered it to be their moral obligation to seek out budding civilizations, and to assist them in becoming citizens of a vast and growing Galactic Society. At the time of their missionary exodus they had established contact with no less than thirty other worlds, many of whom were even more technically and spiritually evolved. Their most distant communion was with a planetary system almost a thousand light-years away! By mutual agreement with the other members of this Galactic Society, Selestia had been assigned the task of searching a specific section of the heavens for any fledgling worlds. The Sun was one star on their list of potential candidates.

During their long association with other worlds the Selestians had learned that actual physical contact, between races of various planetary systems, was fraught with danger. Although all bore a remarkable similarity, each hominoid life form had evolved quite separately, and each had developed immune systems designed to offer protection from specific types of bacteria and viruses. Unfortunately, such protection did not extend to other worlds. For this reason the Selestians had not settled on Earth. They had, however, landed on our planet clad in protective space suits, where they had found encouraging signs of advanced bipedal life. After some study, they finally concluded that it would be prudent to invest time and effort in belief that an intelligent species would one day arise. With this thought in mind they had retreated to Mars and constructed the "Face" - a structure which would be sure to be noticed and investigated by an emerging civilization once they had attained space flight capability.

In expectation that this infant world could benefit from their superior wisdom and technology, they proposed to leave within the "Face" a priceless legacy. The unpressurized outer chamber would contain a capsule intended to convey insight into their language, culture and history. Philosophy and cosmology, along with such sciences as astronomy, physics and biology, were also considered prime subjects appropriate for their purpose. In particular, it was deemed essential to stress the importance of establishing a society based upon equality and unselfishness.

Within the locked inner chamber the Selestians would leave behind many useful machines and devices, including one which would provide safe, cheap, clean and virtually unlimited electrical power. Another secret they offered to share was that of extending life expectancy - by a factor of some three hundred percent! But what really excited the team of linguists, upon decoding a section of the data sheets, was a treatment which could cure all forms of cancer! According to their interpretation of the alien text, it was a machine which emitted a highly unique sequence of radiation pulses that would promptly and totally destroy all malignancies without the slightest harm to healthy tissue.

Earth scientists could hardly wait to avail themselves of the treasures now concealed behind the green door. Nevertheless, when it came to the secret of interstellar space flight, the Selestians were aware of the consequences of placing advanced technology into the hands of a potentially hostile race. This information would not be forthcoming until future contact could justify such trust.

With regard to the issue of contacting other civilizations, the Selestians invited Earth scientists to make every effort to do so. To facilitate this attempt they even listed the common radio band frequency that had been agreed upon by the Galactic Society of Worlds. The data sheets also mentioned that the participants of this Society had managed to develop a universal language - one which the Selestians themselves had chosen to adopt, just a few millennia after having been granted membership in this most elite galactic body. As to the coordinates of these advanced worlds, the information was necessarily vague. Star systems are simply not stationary relative to each other over substantial periods of time. They tend to move in different directions and at different rates of speed. Without accurate knowledge as to when the aliens had left their record inside the "Face," it would be difficult to deduce their present location within the vast expanse of our Milky Way galaxy.

Fortunately, the Selestians had provided a means for them to derive some idea as to the approximate locations of these other worlds. Moreover, it would also afford a way to date any alien artifacts. The clue lay in the positions of the various star constellations which existed at the time the "Face" was carved out of a small and eroded Martian mountain. Imprinted on the arched ceiling of the outer chamber, as well as on pages of the data sheets, were maps of star constellations as seen from Mars at that particular era of time. Earth astronomers, with knowledge of the movement of many of these stars, were soon able to obtain a rough idea as to when the alien charts had been made.

If recent computer simulations were correct, the Selestians must have visited the Solar System somewhere in the neighborhood of 300,000 years ago. According to information, gleaned from the alien records, they had remained for about three hundred Martian years. When they finally resumed their missionary crusade it was to visit nearby alpha Centauri, a G-2 type star some 4.3 light-years distant. Assuming that they spent a similar amount of time in the vicinity of the new system, by now they could be almost anywhere in this quadrant of the Milky Way.

Facilitating their lengthy voyages of exploration was a huge saucer-shaped spaceship, powered by several matter/antimatter reactors. Its dimensions, as translated from the alien's text, were an incredible 1,200 meters across by 300 meters at greatest thickness. It carried a complement of approximately 4,000 souls, none of whom would be likely to visit their home world in person. Although greater speeds could be attained, it had been determined that a cruising velocity in excess of 10% light speed was to be avoided. To exceed this figure was to risk serious hull damage through encounters with the interstellar medium, as efficiency of their plasma shields began to drop off rather sharply beyond this point. Warp speed between star systems, in excess of the velocity of light, was an outright physical impossibility. While it made for exciting science fiction, it was clearly a product of man's fertile imagination.

Upon reaching a new solar system, the huge Selestian craft would remain in orbit around a prospective planet. A series of landing parties would then exit the mother ship in smaller shuttle craft and descend to the surface. Clad in protective space suits, as a precaution against mutual contamination, the explorers would make a detailed survey of the various life forms. A report would be beamed back to their home world, where it would subsequently be relayed to other members of the Milky Way's Galactic Society. In this way a comprehensive picture would eventually emerge of all the intelligent (or potentially intelligent) sources of hominoid life in the galaxy. In spite of speculation to the contrary, up until the time that the Selestians had composed the data sheets there was no knowledge of other radically different species of high intelligence. The bipedal form, it appeared, was probably the ultimate matrix for biological life throughout the expanse of the universe.

To many citizens of Earth the existence of great starships, roaming methodically through the heavens, seemed very much like science fiction come true. This impression was even supported by the Selestian's open admission that, while on peaceful missions, such ships were not without a means of defense. They did, in fact, carry an arsenal of powerful laser-type cannon, along with a quantity of matter/antimatter torpedoes. Although prepared for a worst case scenario, it was stressed that no occasion was known where these weapons had ever been deployed against a hostile race. Battles between great starships simply did not occur. Indeed, the exceedingly high degree of technology required would invariably be matched by advanced moral values. For once a civilization reached the Atomic Age it was generally a choice between self-destruction, or promptly developing the ability to live in harmony with one's neighbor.

The starships themselves were virtually entire cities enclosed within thick metallic walls. With the capability of generating prodigious amounts of electrical power, rotation of entire inner sections provided the artificial gravity so essential for lengthy space voyages. Within the closed confines of a perfectly balanced ecological system, it was possible to simulate a most hospitable planetary environment - one devoid of all the pesky and obnoxious organisms that plague worlds teaming with biological life. Common areas were adorned with picturesque streams, ponds, fountains and a profusion of colorful vegetation. Countless generations were born, lived and died within these celestial cities, without any desire to return to their ancestral home. Whatever raw materials they required could be readily obtained from the planets that they visited which, on the average, was every century or so - unless, of course, enticed to stay longer on some promising world.

The Selestian's initial contact, with members of the Galactic Society, had been accomplished by means of the radio telescope. Having reasoned that other intelligent civilizations must populate the Milky Way, they had launched a concerted search with numerous instruments capable of monitoring myriad broadcast channels. Not content to merely listen, they soon began beaming signals of their own to promising star systems. Within the span of a few years they had stumbled upon their first contact: electromagnetic pulses emanating from the vicinity of a star some 120 light-years away. Broadcast upon the specific frequency adopted by members of the Galactic Society, it was obviously not in response to their own recently emitted signals. It was to be over a century before they received a reply to their earlier transmissions.

Once contact had been established it soon became possible to exchange a wealth of information, including video pictures and insight into respective languages. Within a millennium the planet Selestia had received its first visit from one of the great starships. Some three millennia later they were granted admission into the galaxy's elite federation.

The planet Selestia bore an amazing resemblance to Earth. Its oceans swarmed with a rich and almost endless variety of marine life; while its continents featured such forms as mammals, birds, reptiles, amphibians and insects. Likewise, the planet exhibited opposing ice caps and lush tropical vegetation throughout much of its equatorial regions. However, unlike Earth's one large moon, their planet possessed three considerably smaller satellites. In size, they ranged from 300 to 700 km in diameter, and were located at mean distances of 20,000, 45,000 and 80,000 km. Their solar system even contained a number of comparable gas giants, although it possessed only three as opposed to our four.

Evolution of life forms appeared to closely parallel Earth's history. From a microscopic marine origin a great profusion of creatures - including dinosaur-type monstrosities - arose over a period of many hundreds of millions of years. Eventually, bipedal life forms came to be the dominant species on Selestia, just as it had on our own planet. With the passage of time certain hominoids developed into intelligent beings which resembled mankind in every essential aspect. In fact, after studying pictures etched into the plastic/metallic data sheets, scientists were hard pressed to discover a significant distinction from modern man. If anything, they seemed to be a slightly taller and more noble race.

While the history of the Selestian people had a great deal in common with Earth, there were several notable differences. Rising above the primitive tribal state, they likewise proceeded to form themselves into nations and indulged in a succession of kingly rulers. As might be predicted, some were good and others bad - including some who were absolute tyrants. The enlightened concept of democracy, when it did come, was also born of much suffering and strife, eventually being recognized as the only true basis upon which to base a just and stable society.

Emerging from the yoke of emperors and aristocratic rulers, the inhabitants of Selestia began to experiment with governments patterned after the capitalist system of economics. Under the moderating influence of democracy, it was not long before some nations began to smooth a few of the rougher edges by introducing social reforms designed to assist the underprivileged masses. It was at this point that a dichotomy developed in the manner whereby the principle of democracy was practiced, setting the stage for opposing ideologies and the potential for global war.

The first group chose the more liberal path of granting the right to vote merely upon reaching a specific age, without any regard for competence. Since wealth and power were still largely in the hands of a comparatively few, this provided an opportunity to prey upon the minds of the unenlightened. Controlling all the major avenues of information, it was not difficult to manipulate voters into electing one worthless candidate after another. The power of media propaganda was awesome to behold, and it was not long before a handful of wealthy individuals managed to acquire control of entire nations - from a populace that deluded itself into thinking that it was dictating policy just because one was able to cast a ballot.

The second group recognized the folly of allowing all adults - whether highly intelligent or village idiot - the privilege of electing their representatives. Instead, they restricted the right to share a voice in government to those who could pass a stiff test devised to emphasize principles, and to weed out the incompetent and the uninformed - with age, race or sex having nothing whatsoever to do with the issue. Moreover, they freely acknowledged that it is very difficult for democracy to work properly unless there is reasonable equality of wealth. With the advent of such mass media as big newspaper chains, magazines, TV and radio stations, it was necessary for many election candidates to expend huge sums of money to obtain the flattering publicity needed to win an election. Clearly, ability to wage a successful political campaign favored those best able to pay. Only a society whose voters were capable of discerning values and principles may counteract this bias. Only they could resist the temptation to elect a candidate simply because of extensive media endorsement.

Thus it came to pass that the population of Selestia became divided into two opposing camps. This separation was facilitated in some measure by the topography of the planet, which featured two giant land masses sandwiched between even larger oceans. The one continent, known as "Mercano," embraced the selfish philosophy of unrestricted wealth and private ownership of virtually every facet of a nation's economy. The other group, referred to in the alien text as inhabitants of the continent "Harmonia," were the ones that restricted the right to vote. They advocated policies controlling wealth and undertook steps which assured a much more equitable distribution of resources.

In time, a small variation in living standards widened to become a large gap. Where the very idea of public ownership had been viewed with almost fanatical suspicion, a growing imbalance of wealth eventually posed a serious problem. Unable (or simply unwilling) to give the masses adequate purchasing power, the grim specter of high unemployment became rampant. Noting that a strong military economy could siphon off many of the jobless, while the manufacture of expensive armaments would inject large sums into a depressed economy, the Mercanos soon acquired the reputation of being a warlike race. Nor did the unethical practice of resorting to "deficit financing," in order to pay for such expenditures, do much to alleviate matters. Failure to properly tax the rich was tantamount to burdening generations of the poor with a debt that was only aggravated by needless interest charges.

On the other hand, the Harmonians had no such inducement to "make work" by thrusting unemployed youth into armies. (In fact, this very practice was considered to be little more than a savage relapse into slavery!) Their economy quickly evolved into what might be described as a harmonious mixture of free enterprise and democratic socialism. Adopting a tax structure which severely limited personal wealth, an immediate benefit was to finance a truly comprehensive health care plan for only a token payment. While encouraging the operation of modest business concerns, it was nevertheless deemed essential to nationalize all finance, utilities, land development and large industries. They also found it desirable to virtually abolish an old capitalist tradition of charging interest for the use of money. With no reason to borrow funds from private sources, in order to finance housing and public works, the extra purchasing power was passed on to its citizens. Putting the economy on a firm basis by regulating the supply of money in free circulation, so as to always achieve a balance with available consumer's goods, it was possible to create a standard of living which far surpassed that of the Mercanos. Unemployment was completely eliminated by the simple expedient of adjusting the retirement age, so that sufficient jobs were made available for youthful arrivals into the work force. (One always had the option of working or retiring on pension, but never both.)

Compelled for many years to support a volunteer defense force, by way of guarding against the threat of Mercano aggression, the Harmonians were unable to reap the full rewards of their superior economy until the dawn of the Nuclear Age. An almost simultaneous development by both parties, the introduction of atomic weaponry soon made conventional arms and big armies obsolete. As events turned out, this newly released manpower enabled the Harmonians to so widen the gap in living standards that it caused their opponent to take drastic measures.

In an attempt to suppress knowledge of their rival's superior economic system, the Mercano government began to launch a massive propaganda campaign to discredit the Harmonians. Inventing lame excuses, they acted to severely restrict travel and communications between the two continents, lest the truth be spread with rather predictable consequences. More or less sealed within their own borders, and falsely taught to believe that it was their neighbor who posed a threat, generations of Mercanos lived and died without realizing the deception. Those who did speak out against their leaders were promptly branded as traitors and persecuted with considerable vigor. Controlling all facets of the news media, a clique of wealthy individuals managed to dupe a gullible populace into condoning the policies of a succession of worthless election candidates. Thus the stage was set for an impending disaster.

Had it not been for the presence of a large and independent island, situated between the two great land masses, there was no telling how long this isolation might have continued. Eventually, however, circumstances conspired to produce a dangerous situation. When the feared nuclear holocaust did come it was quite unexpected and occurred before diplomats on either side could do very much to avert it.

The point of friction arose shortly after the surprise ending of a general election held on the island of "Kobon," located just seven hundred kilometers from the heavily populated east coast of Mercano. Long controlled by puppets of its powerful neighbor, the new government proceeded to adopt many of the basic reforms of the Harmonians. Alarmed by this sudden turn of events, the Mercano leaders were fearful that such revolutionary tendencies might gain a foothold on the continent itself. The island lay far too close to the mainland and contained far too many relatives of their own people to rely upon the usual propaganda and isolation techniques. The upstarts had to be swiftly removed from office - even if force was required!

When a dastardly assassination campaign produced only minimal results, a powerful invasion fleet was dispatched. Counting on the pacifistic nature of the Harmonians not to intervene in this action, the Mercano military leaders felt confident that they could seize control of the entire island in just a few days. In such an assumption they were to be proven correct; for as much as their rival deplored this blatant act of aggression they dared not risk all for the sake of one small nation.

What had been overlooked, in their nefarious scheme, was the resourcefulness of the Kobons themselves in devising a hasty but effective plan of defense. Anticipating just such a reaction, once their intentions were revealed, they had surreptitiously planted a number of H-bombs in the harbor areas of major Mercano seaports. No less than a dozen were even carried far inland and concealed in buildings at the centers of most of their principal cities. By the time the invasion fleet approached their shores the Kobons had a potent deterrent at their disposal.

Issuing an ultimatum to the Mercanos to withdraw their fleet, or suffer annihilation of a specified coastal city, the new island leaders truly believed that their former allies would listen to reason. Unfortunately, the invaders thought it was all a bluff designed to stall for time while help was being sought from the Harmonians. Upon evacuating much of the city in question, the Mercanos pressed home their attack with all possible haste. With knowledge of the few island missile sites, they unleashed a deluge of rockets. In short order their nuclear warheads eliminated the only positively known retaliatory threat.

At this point the Kobons decided that they had no choice but to show that they meant business by exploding the H-bomb in the prescribed area, obliterating the seaport in a blinding flash. Angered, the Mercanos responded by flattening their antagonist's capitol city. The fat was now in the fire. The Kobons threatened to detonate three more bombs if Mercano leaders would not agree to immediately cease hostilities, and to resign from office. Quite unwilling to accept either demand, their vastly superior force stormed ashore. Within minutes the three targeted Mercano cities were little more than piles of smouldering rubble. Retaliation was swift and decisive, as the invaders proceeded to wipe out every town and city on the island. In their death throes the Kobons triggered the remainder of their concealed nuclear bombs, inflicting far greater loss of lives and property.

Assessing the fearful price of victory, the Mercano military chiefs proposed sending an ultimatum to the despised Harmonians, who appeared to be the only winner in the carnage that had just ensued. Even though half the continent lay in ruins, it was a fact that their nuclear strike force was fully intact. Besides, with so much more to lose, there was a good chance that their arch rival would capitulate rather than risk far higher casualties and damage beyond what they might expect to impose, in return, upon an already partially devastated nation.

Perhaps it was the personal loss of friends and relatives that caused the Mercano president to once again lose his sanity; for he sanctioned the diabolical plan. In any event, when the Harmonians refused to yield to surrender demands he ordered the launching of a full scale missile attack. After the inevitable retaliation materialized the fate of the entire planet was placed in jeopardy. At least six hundred nuclear devices had been exploded, leaving Selestia in utter ruins. Its once proud cities reduced to rubble, and with barely ten percent of its population managing to survive the radiation sickness and pestilence which followed, prophecy was now a stark reality.

For many years their philosophers had warned of the danger if positive steps toward global disarmament were not given highest priority. There had been much talk but no action until, at last, time had simply run out on them. Both the just and the unjust alike had paid the supreme penalty for the selfishness of a group of wealthy individuals who had refused to yield to the interest of society. It would be a great many years before any recovery would be possible.

Clearly, this saga of nuclear savagery was a dark blot on the planet's history, affording a most valuable lesson which could never be forgotten. It was the fervent hope of the Selestians that their story would serve as a dire warning to other emerging civilizations.

Chapter 6

REVELATION AND REACTION

While the early economic and political history of Selestia may have had much in common with that of Earth, there was a notable difference when it came to such issues as religion and philosophy. During both their Stone Age and a subsequent Bronze Age they had likewise entertained notions of a variety of gods, in an attempt to explain a universe that was totally beyond their comprehension. At the beginning of the Industrial Age the idea of a single and all-powerful Creator had virtually replaced previous inventions of multiple deities. By the dawn of the Atomic Age this concept had given way to the view that the entire universe was more likely the product of some great overall *Cosmic Scheme* or *Principle.*

Initial thoughts concerning the possibility of a life after death predated the Selestian's Stone Age, according to impressive archeological evidence in the form of artifacts found buried with their primitive ancestors. Following invention of the microscope and telescope, and with the advent of somewhat advanced logic, the principle of hominoid reincarnation was expanded to embrace a more universal outlook. Instead of just a privileged species that was blessed with such potential, it was recognized that there could be no exclusions - invariably, it had to be a case of *all or nothing!* Selestian philosophers were unanimous in choosing the former. At no point in their intellectual history did they seriously consider the notion of a Creator appearing in hominoid form! Nor was there mention of any other civilization that had done so.

As knowledge of the physical universe increased, so did they come to a better understanding of the vital role that must surely be played by reincarnation in the process of cosmic evolution. As events turned out, one of their scientist's greatest discoveries was derived from an extrapolation of philosophical theory. Noting a rather curious mathematical relationship between phenomena of the ultra-large and the ultra-small, along with the necessity of having to include even the smallest quantum of mass/energy in any scheme of universal reincarnation, they inadvertently stumbled upon the formula for describing the repulsive factor which had long been suspected to be inherent in gravitation.

A treatise of Selestian cosmology/philosophy, as decoded by the International Team, was given wide publicity by the various news media. Highlights of this Big Picture, which tended to very much substantiate and enlarge upon many of Professor Duncan's views, was published in the *Vero Beach Gazette.* A synopsis of this article follows:

The Selestians looked upon the universe as a dynamic Spiritual Pyramid, in which myriad swarms of infinitesimal entities at the bottom are able to achieve a constant reduction of numbers through the process of *fusion,* as they steadily evolve to higher levels - with one entire level of spirit/energy at the apex fused together to form *One Harmonious Whole: God!*

Realizing that the expansion velocity of the universe must be determined by both the rate of continuous creation and the rate of spiritual evolution, they inferred that any distance/repulsion (D/R) aspect of gravitation is closely related to the total amount of matter in the universe, and to the quantity of "A" (a symbol used to depict the smallest unit of creation) deduced to be locked up in nature's ultimate atomic particle: a proton. It remained only to state this relationship in mathematical terms.

Although 20th century Earth physicists had been aware of four ultra-large/ultra-small relationships - involving the immense sum of 10^{40} - the Selestians knew of five. The fifth was the initial ratio of repulsion to attraction, inherent in a proton, expressed over a distance equal to that of its diameter. Such relationships may be stated as follows:

(1) At really close proximity, the electrical charge of a positive/negative pair of particles exceeds the combined force of their gravitational influence by a factor of very nearly 10^{40}.

(2) The density ratio of highly degenerate stars, as compared with the average density of matter throughout the expanse of the universe, is of the order of 10^{40}.

(3) Stretched out in a straight line, like a string of beads, it would take about 10^{40} protons to reach the distance at which the galaxies are receding at the speed of light.

(4) The square root of the number of protons, within range of our observable universe, (10^{80}) is none other than 10^{40}.

(5) The repulsive aspect of gravitation, at a distance equal to the diameter of a "maximum" particle, is seen to be some 10^{20} times weaker than attraction - in essence, such repulsion is the square root of attraction.

Whereas gravitational attraction obeys the well-known inverse-square law (i.e. a twofold increase of distance results in a fourfold reduction of strength), the inferred D/R force increases by a factor of two with each fourfold increase of distance - exactly the reverse case scenario of attraction! From a starting point of the order of a proton's diameter (about $1.5x10^{-13}$ cm), the formula implies a repulsive force becoming equal to that of attraction at a distance of roughly 17 million light-years - beyond which all galactic systems are induced to partake in the expansion of the universe. As Earth astronomers were forced to very reluctantly concede, such a repulsive force could well explain a number of rather vexing "missing mass" problems. It also spelled finish to all notions of a Big Bang philosophy!

In assessing the reason for this curious 10^{40} relationship, the Selestians chose to explain it as an expression of *fusion versus non-fusion.* With gravitation viewed as an expression of the inborn desire of all components of creation to evolve through the process of fusion, it is a reflection of a particle's ability to achieve communion with the universe as a whole. By contrast, the electrical charge of a material particle is a manifestation of this same worth condensed to a volume of space equal to that of its immediate self: the halo of energy surrounding the particle in question. Since there is good reason to believe that the value of "A" fused within a proton does not exceed that of its halo by an exorbitant figure, it follows that exposure to another charged particle will produce a magnified reaction that is essentially in proportion to the quantity of "A" involved. Hence, it is to be presumed that roughly 10^{40} "A"s are likely fused within a proton.

A philosophical basis for the inferred D/R factor would thus seem implicit in theory. It is surely more than a coincidence that, at the point where this repulsive force is first able to manifest itself, it does so as the square root of the number of fused "A"s which are believed to constitute a "maximum" particle. Indeed, it is essential that a two-fold increase in the strength of repulsion induce a fourfold increase of distance in order for nature to achieve a balance between the rate of new creation and the rate of cosmic evolution. In effect, *the time scale of our expanding universe is determined directly by the rate of spiritual advancement!*

With a total of 10^{80} protons comprising our physical universe, and 10^{40} fused "A"s per proton, it will be deduced that Perfection - or any one "level" within the Great Cosmic Pyramid - is equal to some 10^{120} "A"s. In terms of spiritual evolution this Ultimate State would involve approximately 400 "steps," or occasions of doubling. Subsequently, an entity of the status of a proton is assumed to reside 1/3rd of the way toward the top of the Pyramid, having already climbed some 133 "steps" from its origin as a lowly "A". Upon this premise, slightly less than one percent of all the mass-energy in the universe is likely to be incorporated into stable material particles.

A most intriguing prospect which now surfaces involves our ability to determine the universal "time constant" that must surely regulate the entire process of spiritual fusion. For it is an integral feature of theory that all levels of spirit must be capable of doubling their worth in some common interval of time. A solution to this problem will make it possible to derive a most useful picture as to the average time that an individual must serve in order to achieve one doubling of status. Moreover, it will also provide insight into the highly relevant question as to when one might expect a future rebirth.

In converting all subsequent discussion of this time aspect to terms of Earth evolution, one is led to consider certain factors. For instance, the rate of disintegration (at the periphery of the universe) must be included in any equation attempting to express events in terms of a human lifetime. Due to a steady annihilation of worlds containing the various life forms, there will prevail a situation in which disrupted levels of spirit are compelled to seek rebirth on appropriate planets still residing within the Cosmic Creation Zone. Along with other factors pointing toward a similar conclusion, this introduces the suspicion that, in terms of the world with which a spirit was last associated, considerable time could elapse between reincarnations. In effect, biological evolution is likely to reflect a "sharing" of available body-forms with displaced spirit from alien planets - with the result that spiritual entities are, for all intents and purposes, excused from having a physical manifestation over most of a world's lengthy history. (Time, of course, simply does not exist for spirit that is between incarnations, just as it appears to cease when we fall into a deep and dreamless sleep.)

Thus, in theory, it could follow that those who succeed in increasing their intrinsic worth, in excess of the average, will receive the equivalent of a longer postponement in their next rebirth - thereby enhancing the likelihood of securing existence in more suitable surroundings. On the other hand, one who has made relatively little or no progress (whether or not restricted by premature death) may expect to be reborn in but a fraction of this time and, if so justified, in a less favorable environment. Perhaps, in this manner, nature permits us some latitude with regard to determining the circumstances into which we are reborn - including the specific moment of rebirth within an evolutionary era. Most assuredly, there is a great advantage to be gained from being reincarnated in a more advanced and civilized age.

Clearly, the *rate of expansion* of the universe must constitute a key factor in any approach to the time aspect of evolution. Why do galaxy clusters double their separations in an interval of some 12 billion years? Why this particular figure? Obviously, the greater the rate of expansion the greater the disintegration at the edge of the universe. Inasmuch as this annihilation factor must be balanced through creation - in order that mass-energy may be conserved - it will be seen that the introduction and evolution of new "A" is closely related to the recession of the galaxies. The issue, therefore, is basically one of determining precisely how this "A" is introduced with respect to each cycle of Hubble's constant (i.e. rate of expansion of the universe).

Upon due consideration, the one logical possibility to emerge would seem to embrace the premise that *one entire level of new "A" is created in just such a span of time, and is able to fulfill its destiny by evolving to a state of Perfection in this very same interval!* Should this be the case it must follow that the time required by spirit, to double its worth, may be determined through dividing Hubble's constant by the number of "steps" or doublings separating "A" from Perfection.

Assuming a proton to consist of 10^{40} "A"s, and a physical universe of 10^{80} protons, we have a spiritual pyramid of some 10^{120} "A"s per level and a total of approximately 400 "steps." Notwithstanding the possibility of other universes, in view of the most unique relationship of the sum of 10^{40}, as it relates to the size of our finite universe, along with the inability of material forms to communicate in excess of light speed, it is perhaps in order to treat such a region as though it were a complete system terminating in what - for all practical purposes - we may describe as God. Subsequently, a period of roughly 30 million years per occasion of doubling may be derived.

Proceeding upon this basis, it will now be deduced that only 1/400th of an entire level of new "A" will be created in a period of 30 million years. In effect, this means that only one spirit entity in 400 may have a "conscious" (or physical) manifestation at any given instant. But if 30 million years is the allotted time, in which one *entire* level of spirit must double its status, this restriction will introduce an additional factor of 400 into the time permitted for actual instances of physical incarnation. Dividing our 30 million year period by this further factor of 400, we are left with about 75,000 years as the average elapsed time for a "conscious" existence between doublings.

Yet another factor is imposed by disintegration at the edge of the universe, as displaced spirit must periodically be reborn within the Cosmic Creation Zone. Since it takes time for stars and planets to form and evolve biological entities, it is evident that this factor is very much related to status. Calculation of the average age of matter, within the framework of a Steady-state cosmology, yields the information that only one part in 20 will be as old as Hubble's constant.

Upon this line of reasoning the average time required by all spirit - as a "conscious" entity - to double in value may well be expressed by the formula:

$$T = \frac{SH}{DLS^2} \quad \text{or:} \quad T = \frac{H}{DLS}$$

Where:

T = Time required to achieve one doubling of status in terms of a "conscious" existence.

S = Total number of cosmic "steps" from "A" to Perfection (or Full Communion) within a finite physical universe some 18 BLY in radius.

H = Hubble's constant (deduced to be about 12 BY).

D = Disintegration factor (at the edge of the universe) in one cycle of Hubble's constant.

L = Level of spirit in question (defined in terms of the total number of "steps" evolved beyond the initial state of "A").

Assuming that 400 "steps" extend between "A" and Perfection, it now becomes essential to determine the position of mankind in this overall scheme. With a hydrogen atom established at "step" 133, this problem may well be resolved by a comparison of the relative abundance of the proton to man throughout the universe.

By way of assessing this ratio it may be estimated that about 10^{22} Earth-type planets presently exist in the universe, of which only about one in 10^{5} will currently feature biological evolution equivalent to man at his present level. Multiplying our estimated 10^{17} planets by the sum of 10^{10} (representing an average long-term population of man per planet), we arrive at a total of 10^{27} human beings at this particular level. Since some 10^{80} protons are held to constitute our physical universe, we may deduce a ratio of about 10^{53} protons for every man. Translated into "steps" in the Cosmic Pyramid, this sum is equal to some 177 doublings. Hence, the level of man may be derived by adding these 177 "steps" to the 133 "steps" believed to characterize a proton - leading one to the conclusion that man presently resides at about the 310th "step."

With this information we may now attempt to solve the "time constant" for man as per formula. Therefore:

$$T = \frac{12{,}000{,}000{,}000}{20 \times 310 \times 400} = 4{,}800 \text{ years (approximately)}$$

Thus it would be calculated that, upon the average, man must serve a total of something like 4,800 years (or about 70 lifetimes of 70 years) in order to double his intrinsic worth. (It will be noted that any uncertainty in computing the ratio of man to proton will not seriously alter our estimate, since an error by a factor of a million will only make a difference of about 6%; while an almost inconceivable million million would be merely 12%!)

With insight into man's status in the Cosmic Pyramid, along with knowledge of the "time constant" of spiritual fusion, we may now face the issue of reincarnation in terms of Earth evolution. During what past age did we last live? Moreover, in what future era are we likely to be reborn?

Considering the necessity of accommodating displaced spirit from other worlds, along with the overall cycle of doubling which is of the order of 30 million years, reincarnation may essentially take the form of a projection well into the future and into the confines of another planetary environment! Thus, if man requires 4,800 years as a "conscious" existence to achieve one doubling of status over a period of 30 million years, it will be tantamount to an elapsed time of almost 6,200 years for each year of a past life. Based upon an average life expectancy of 70 years, this would call for a rebirth some four to five hundred thousand years into the future. However, if only 1/400th of an entire level of "A" is created per 30 million year cycle, in terms of Earthly evolution the *apparent* elapsed time will be less than the *actual* time by this very same factor. Subsequently, for all intents and purposes, the reincarnation of man may be linked to the formula:

$$R = \frac{YH}{TS^2}$$

The two additional symbols may be defined as follows:

R = Rebirth of man (in years) in terms of a future era on Earth.

Y = The number of years lived during last incarnation.

Hence: $$R = \frac{70 \times 12{,}000{,}000{,}000}{4{,}800 \times 400 \times 400} = 1{,}100 \text{ years (approx)}$$

In other words, what may very well transpire is that a man is actually reborn some hundreds of thousands of years from now; but in relation to the environmental status with which he was last associated, it will be equivalent to an evolutionary era only a thousand years or so into the future.

Upon contemplating the future of mankind, as a biological species, it may be theorized that each additional doubling will require some 75,000 years in terms of Earth evolution. The eventual passage of man, beyond his present transitory and rather frail human form, could conceivably have a solution in such an astronomical curiosity as a stellar black hole (or neutron star?) - essentially, a *super atomic particle!* Best described as an immense concentration of mass-energy contracted into virtual spatial oblivion, the ratio of mankind to such totally fused objects should permit computation of the number of "steps" needed to achieve this inferred evolution. With this being the case, it may indeed be said that man's destiny is to be found in the stars!

Not only does this black hole state of matter possess all the required attributes of a "super particle" spiritual entity, but an excellent agreement of numbers would appear to connect theory with observation. It is surely more than a mere coincidence that an estimate, of all the stellar black holes likely to exist in the universe, should coincide with the probable number of Earth-type planets that are allowed to fulfill their evolutionary roles. Moreover, it can be shown that the quantity of "A" fused within a typical stellar black hole (some 10^{58} protons x 10^{40} "A"s, or some 10^{98} fused "A"s), when multiplied by the number of such objects in the entire universe, is very likely of the same order as the total spiritual worth (or "A" content) of one complete population of our present day Earth-man multiplied by the quantity of all existing worlds of a similar evolutionary level. The implication is little short of obvious: *A stellar black hole may well constitute the eventual destiny of a humanity, so deserving of intimate harmony, as to become fused into a new entity of truly enormous magnitude!*

By way of determining the number of cosmic "steps," between current man and the exalted status of a stellar black hole, it is necessary to examine what transpires as man finally evolves beyond his present level, which we might define as M^1. Upon doubling his worth, and attaining the status of M^2, it will be noted that a gap has suddenly appeared in our planet's otherwise unbroken chain of evolutionary life forms. In effect, there is no longer any level recognizable as M^1. Similarly, after M^2 progresses to the status of M^3, the gap will widen to include the absence of both M^1 and M^2 levels. For the first time in our planet's history a gap has been produced in the evolutionary continuum - one that will continue to grow in size until mankind's eventual extinction as a biological entity! Assuming that only about one Earth-type planet in 10^5 will feature human life equivalent to a specific "M" level, it may be deduced that some 17 doublings will suffice to accomplish the inferred evolution from M^1 to the status of a stellar black hole. Accordingly, this momentous stage may be looked upon as "step" 327 in a Cosmic Pyramid of 400 "steps."

The significance of this 17 "step" gap, in the evolutionary sequence of all Earth-type planets, lies in its ability to resolve a paradox with regard to a final merger of spirit into a stellar black hole. Without the existence of this gap, which must result in the black holes outnumbering any one specific "M" level by a factor of 10^5, we would encounter a somewhat outlandish situation at the more advanced stages of man's evolution. Since theory demands a reduction of numbers in direct proportion to higher status, it follows that the final "M" stages would otherwise be quite literally populated by a mere handful of individuals. The inferred gap of some 17 "steps" will greatly alleviate such a problem by assuring that the ultimate "M" stage, immediately prior to achieving stellar black hole fusion, will consist of not less than 10^5 spiritual entities. When combined with the ratio of 10^5 stellar black holes in excess of a solitary "M" stage, we arrive at a total of 10^{10} entities - exactly the sum needed to account for a typical M^1 population level! No wonder there is a curious similarity in the numbers of stellar black holes and Earth-type planets. It does, in fact, seem to necessitate a "surplus" of 10^5 stellar black holes in order to balance cosmic books in terms of "A" content.

To grasp the full picture of this "M" stage gap it will be noted that, immediately prior to our present level, there is an abrupt increase (10^5) in worlds which must require a corresponding reduction in the numbers of pre-human entities in order to comply with theory. This is precisely what is observed when we examine the distribution of our own terrestrial life forms. The relative shortage of primitive man is clearly no accident. Nor is the recent sharp increase in human population an unprecedented event. In both instances we are likely witnessing nature's balancing of appropriate cosmic equations. (Incidently, it may be said that the comparative scarcity of early man tends to substantiate the contention that there is really little difference in spiritual value between the higher animals and primitive man - with the family pet possibly only short steps away in the evolutionary ladder.)

In predicting the future of mankind, as he passes through successive "M" levels, it is to be inferred that each doubling of worth will involve about 75,000 years in terms of Earth history. After all 17 "M" levels (or generations of human doubling) have been attained, it may be calculated that some 1,275,000 years will have elapsed as mankind finally concludes his evolutionary saga on the planet Earth. From this point onward our world will continue to feature all present life forms below that of M^1; but any trace of a higher intelligence will likely be quite conspicuous by its absence. In actuality, *man will have vanished from the face of this planet simply because he succeeded in evolving beyond the human form!* (This deduction would readily explain any difficulty in contacting beings on other planets. It is not so much that they are intrinsically scarce, as it is that large numbers of such civilizations have already come and gone in the relatively short time span allocated for human supremacy!)

Beyond the lofty status of a stellar black hole lies another cosmos embracing new and unfamiliar laws. Within this world of Principle, spirit is enabled to climax its lengthy evolution by transcending such mundane attributes as gravitation, electricity and time. In the eyes of mortal man the black hole state must be worshipped as a wondrous God-like realm of reciprocal communion - from whence Perfection will ultimately ensue as Total Fusion of Black Hole Minds becomes a reality and time ceases to exist. Somehow, as a direct consequence of this momentous transition from a world of imperfection and time, the mass-energy so released is manifested as a new generation of "A" within the confines of our physical universe.

While many unanswered questions still remain, a truly amazing picture begins to emerge as to what lies beyond the human form. We are at last in a position to glimpse a glorious future that must exceed our wildest dreams. The challenge to comprehend is clearly without parallel; but the reward for crossing this new and highly promising threshold of inquiry will certainly justify the efforts of our best philosophers and scientists.

According to the Selestian data sheets, it was the unifying power of their common philosophical views which saw them through the dark days following the Great Holocaust. With no conflicting religious dogma to set them apart, they had every incentive to work together in harmony in an effort to rebuild their shattered planet. The price of acquiring intelligence had been fearful; but they had learned a lesson to end all lessons.

If one fact was clear to the survivors, it was that individual nations could no longer be permitted to divide their civilization. Nationalism had been revealed to be exactly what it is: a vain and foolish self-centered pride in one's country - an emotion which unscrupulous leaders have fostered so well for their own selfish ends. Only a World Government would allow them to carry out the many major reforms advocated by their more astute philosophers and politicians. High on the agenda was an urgent need for complete disarmament, a common language and an economy in which all of the planet's resources would be shared in an equitable manner.

Forming a small but well-equipped volunteer army from the citizens of all former nations, the Selestians gave first priority to the destruction of any remaining nuclear devices. Effective safeguards were promptly established to assure that no diversion of vital ingredients would ever be used to construct another bomb. Their next step was to launch a vigorous campaign to gather up a wide assortment of conventional weapons scattered throughout the expanse of the planet. It would not be an easy task, but by means of a combination of rewards and penalties it was hoped that the vast majority of arms would be turned in for disposal. The principle of a military draft, so readily tolerated by governments in the past, was strictly outlawed and viewed as a serious crime against both society and the sanctity of conscience. Fortunately, the inhabitants of Selestia were now ready to listen to reason.

When it came to the issue of language, the aliens had a very definite advantage over their Earth counterparts. Instead of babbling in more than a hundred obscure tongues, by the time of the disastrous war the Selestians had reduced their total to a mere handful. A concerted effort was made to incorporate the best features of all languages into one common and unifying tongue. Within a few generations this noble goal was achieved, remaining the planet's sole language until several millennia after they had established contact with other members of the Galactic Society.

The Selestian's program for global economic reform was based on the premise that gross inequality of wealth was at the root of all their troubles. While quick to acknowledge that it would be an injustice to give every citizen the same income, it was also agreed that drastic measures were needed to rectify a situation that had gotten completely out of control over the years. It was finally decided to limit individual wealth to ten times that of the mean yearly wage, with any excess simply becoming the property of the State. In similar fashion, their tax structure was revised to limit the income of all citizens to no more than four times the planetary average. Although these limitations were conceded to be arbitrary in nature, it did prove to be effective in stabilizing the planet's economy. Likewise, the democratic process was to profit by these restrictions, as it served to greatly reduce the usual procession of incompetent and selfish election candidates.

Along with this more equitable distribution of wealth came a necessity to address the issue of public ownership versus the capitalist doctrine of free enterprise. How much of the economy should be allowed to remain in private hands? With no extremely wealthy class to form large corporations of their own, virtually all major industries were restricted to public control. To assure that they were run efficiently, all top supervisory staff were elected to office and subject to periodic review by a panel of employee representatives and government officials. Bereft of the waste imposed by pointless duplication, advertising and model change merely for the sake of change, it was not long before such advantages were found to far outweigh any disadvantages. On the other hand, private ownership of small business concerns was strongly encouraged. Indeed, with public control of finance it was possible for them to escape the burden of having to pay out large sums of money in the form of unnecessary interest charges.

All things considered, this blend of opposing economic systems was reported to be a great success, proving to many Earth politicians that the best solution to a problem might well be a compromise.

Yet another lesson that could be learned from the Selestians turned out to be their sensible method of dealing with criminals. By the dawn of their Atomic Age they had already progressed beyond the crude stage of jail sentences and the death penalty. Whereas Earth society still allowed itself to be victimized twice (once by the original crime and again through having to spend large sums to incarcerate the prisoner), they had a much better solution. Their prisons were actually heavily guarded factories and farms. Paid a competitive wage, the vast bulk of their earnings was deducted for such purposes as room and board, support of their children, and compensation to victims. If a prisoner refused to work or failed to perform properly, for no valid reason, then one simply did not eat. In cases of murder, where the death penalty was thought to be warranted, the prisoner was given the option of State approved suicide. With all prisoners assigned by law to separate quarters, those sentenced to a "suicide cell" would always have access to a "poison pill," located in a special cabinet inside such cells. If one should decide to choose death over a lifetime of daily public servitude, then it was the individual's privilege to do so at any time. When a silent alarm went off, upon opening the cabinet, no guard would hasten to interfere.

Placing great emphasis upon quality rather than quantity of life, the Selestians adopted a very liberal attitude toward the issue of abortion. Having never seriously considered a popular Earth notion that a human "soul" is created at the instant of conception, the termination of a microscopic life form appeared no different than the myriad numbers of other body cells which are born and which die every single day. According to their beliefs, a "soul" is permitted manifestation only after an appropriate brain pattern has evolved - an interval measured in months and not in a split second! In any event, the question of when a "soul" is acquired was deemed merely academic. What was seen to be of prime importance is what happens to a prematurely displaced spiritual entity. To think that it perishes was to deny the existence of a Just Creator. Since it was clear to the Selestians that the very principle of reincarnation assured rebirth into another and quite similar body-form, their chief consideration was the health and future prospects of the unborn embryo.

In this last regard, the aliens were eventually motivated to implement a drastic birth control policy - one designed to filter out serious inherited defects. With their medical scientists extending the lives of many who would otherwise not live beyond puberty, a host of genetically transmitted diseases were allowed to escape nature's own method of containment and be passed on to their children. For this reason they found it expedient to issue birth licenses to prospective parents who had successfully passed the prescribed tests. Failure to comply was to risk State ordered sterilization. The right of an infant to be born healthy and free of preventable inherited defects was considered a principle to be upheld over the callous desires of those who would ignore this very real threat to degrade the planet's genetic pool.

Initial reaction of Earth society to information gleaned from the Selestian data sheets was one of utter amazement. It also held high expectation for the masses. Clearly, the promise of a cure for cancer, a much increased life span and a revolutionary new power source were treasures beyond price. There was certainly no question but what another expedition to Mars would have to be launched just as soon as possible. After giving the matter some thought, project engineers set a target date for the return trip: the year 2044 A.D. Until then, an aroused populace would have to be content with the wealth of knowledge conveyed in records of the alien's history and philosophy.

Unfortunately, not all inhabitants of Earth shared this great enthusiasm. While the vast majority of intelligent citizens were positively ecstatic over the astonishing turn of events, there were certain groups who saw a serious threat to their cherished beliefs. In particular, most adherents to orthodox religions were left in a state of shock over the revelations now made public. To them, it was almost tantamount to denying the existence of God, so entwined had their theology become with the concept of a nebulous Christ/Jesus/God dogma. The very foundation of Christianity and Islam - including Jewish tradition - seemed threatened and likely to fall by the wayside in the face of these new developments. The pope, along with leaders of a number of other popular religious sects, promptly called emergency meetings to discuss what might be done to offset this damaging heresy. They were not at all happy with the fruits of the first expedition to Mars. One could only imagine their fear at the thought of what secrets might lie beyond the sealed green door. It was one thing for an adroit apologist to explain away or degrade mere ideas; it was quite another to deny the reality of more advanced civilizations in the face of a host of miraculous physical devices!

Nor were religious factions the sole parties to be concerned over contents of the Selestian records. The history of the alien planet revealed a close parallel with current economic trends on Earth. It was not difficult to see how many "have-not" nations and individuals here at home might react to the Selestian's story of nuclear holocaust. To the wealthy and powerful elite of Earth the very idea of having to relinquish the bulk of their assets, for the sake of harmony, was quite repugnant to them. In spite of obvious benefits from knowledge of the alien's impressive science and technology, for many it seemed too great a sacrifice to pay. In the eyes of such selfish souls the recent expedition to Mars had all the aspects of a financial catastrophe!

Curiously, not every scientist was delighted at what had been found inside the Martian "Face." Although not nearly so perturbed as the rich and certain religious fundamentalists, not a few of Earth's physicists, astronomers and cosmologists were happy about the loss of prestige as their pet theories were revealed to be in error. It would not be easy for a number of esteemed professors to admit, before an audience of peers and students, that they had been hopelessly wrong. Such, however, is the way that the double-edged sword of truth often cuts.

Chapter 7

RETURN TO MARS: 2044 A.D.

The main observation lounge aboard Space Station Prometheus afforded an excellent view of certain portions of the heavens. Located in the rim of the rotating wheel, it tended to resemble a revolving restaurant turned on its axis. With artificial gravity generated by means of centrifugal force, the outer wall of the rim necessarily became the floor. Windows on opposite sides of the compartment provided contrasting scenes. At the extreme corner of one window the Earth could be glimpsed, its curvature conspicuous in the bright sunshine which bathed the planet's surface. On the other side a black sky predominated, permeated by numerous tiny points of light and a crescent Moon.

Seated about a circular table fastened to the floor, in a simulated gravity of almost one-half "G," were three astronauts awaiting word to transfer into the glistening spacecraft which floated a few hundred meters away. Adam Thompson was the only one of the group that had been a member of the first expedition to Mars, some four years earlier. Seated close beside him, in swivel chairs also connected to the floor, were a husband and wife team: Professor Matthew Duncan and his bride for the past three years, Erica Williams. Their eyes were focused on a large video screen before them.

"I simply fail to understand the mentality of some people," said Erica, wincing at the sight of yet another radio telescope lying in tangled ruins.

"This makes six in as many weeks," stated Thompson, thoroughly disgusted at this latest display of violence.

"I'm afraid it's a case of plain fear," voiced the professor. "I swear that common sense takes a vacation when one's religious beliefs are threatened."

"Two security guards were shot to death and two others are in serious condition," reported the TV commentator.

"Obviously, these terrorists will stop at nothing to achieve their purpose: preventing direct contact with other civilizations beyond our Solar System," remarked Erica.

"What makes it even worse is the way this insanity has spread to so many nations," said Thompson. "There has to be an organized plot behind this madness."

"A really disturbing thought is that this same fanatical group would almost certainly want to sabotage our return mission to the Red Planet," opined the professor.

At this point the trio was joined by a fourth member of the expedition, Brian T. Hawkins, one of two physicists assigned to the mission. England's contribution to the venture, the likeable scientist sported a brief mustache and was the most diminutive male member of the crew, standing 5'-7" tall and weighing a mere 135 lbs. Some 35 years old, he was married and the father of a young son.

"Please join us," said Thompson, motioning to a vacant seat at his side.

"We were just discussing the latest terrorist attack, and of the possibility of such a group wanting to sabotage our mission," said Erica.

"I'm told that security is on top of the situation," commented Hawkins, seating himself next to Adam Thompson, the duly appointed leader of the second expedition to Mars.

"Unfortunately, the problem is far from simple," Thompson was quick to reply. "Not only do we have an unknown number of crazy fanatics masquerading under the guise of religion, but we also have the wealthy to worry about. A great many multimillionaire opponents of the dreaded principle of socialism are undoubtedly shaking in their boots and cursing the day we ever decided to go to the planet Mars."

"When it comes to making enemies, it seems that we have opened up a veritable Pandora's box in finding the Selestian artifacts," remarked Professor Duncan.

"If ever a mission was vulnerable to sabotage it is bound to be ours," Erica declared. "When you consider all of the highly sophisticated components of our spacecraft, it is little short of a minor miracle if nothing goes wrong. Include the possibility of concealed tampering and the potential for failure becomes cause for alarm."

"I hate to mention this unpublicized news item, but I have it on good authority that a saboteur was recently caught in the act of tampering with a strategic valve in our landing craft's lower stage," Thompson announced.

Conversation ceased rather abruptly in response to a program which appeared on the video screen. It was an interview with the world's most popular TV evangelist, Graham W.B. James, commenting on the threat posed to Christianity by the Selestian data sheets. Urging his many followers to uphold the faith in the face of such adversity, he vigorously proclaimed the whole episode of alien contact to be a colossal hoax! The supposed find inside the "Face" was all a diabolical plot, he maintained, produced within the walls of a movie set and designed to discredit Christian theology. Only when the astronauts could bring back genuine physical artifacts of a technology, well beyond that of Earth's 21st century, would he believe in the existence of other worlds and other civilizations.

"I see a man with a lot to lose if we are successful and manage to return with impressive Selestian artifacts," Hawkins commented.

"Which makes me wonder why he would go out on a limb with such a statement. Does he know something we don't?" asked Thompson.

"This incredible hoax theory seems to be spreading," remarked Professor Duncan. "Some months ago I heard the very same wild accusation from the leader of one of the radical Islamic sects. Furthermore, at least one wealthy industrialist has expressed similar sentiments. If any sabotage plot exists it need not be restricted to a single group."

"Oh, great!" exclaimed Erica. "Both the influential rich and the religious crackpots are against us. I sure hope they don't get together and pool their resources."

"Does anyone know what the latest odds are of us bringing back the bacon?" inquired Hawkins.

Further discussion was cut short by an announcement over the station's intercom system. It requested all Mars-bound astronauts to report to docking bay number two, located at the central hub of Prometheus. The time for departure was now at hand.

"This is it, fellow adventurers," declared Thompson, rising from his seat and moving toward the entrance of a nearby spoke which linked the hub to the revolving rim.

Entering the tube, the four astronauts proceeded along the passageway which led to the docking area. As they approached the hub they could feel a marked reduction in the strength of their artificially induced gravity. Upon reaching the central hub they would be floating in an essentially weightless state.

At the end of the connecting tube they emerged into a spacious compartment where they were greeted by the other members of the expedition, along with a video news camera recording the historic event. Introducing the twelve astronauts chosen to participate in a return to Mars, the TV commentator conveyed a much abbreviated profile of each crew member to his audience. Essentials of these statistics are as follows:

Adam Thompson: 39-year-old veteran American pilot, 6'-2" tall, 180 lbs, married with two children. By reason of impressive credentials and his experiences on the initial voyage to the Red Planet, he became the unanimous choice as mission leader. He was also the only member of the first expedition scheduled to make the return trip.

Matthew Duncan: 37-year-old Canadian professor of linguistics and philosophy, 5'-10" tall, 170 lbs, married with no children. In view of his extensive knowledge of the Selestian's language, and considering the great necessity of including such an expert to decode alien text to be found inside the "Face," he was a logical candidate for the mission.

Erica Duncan: 31-year-old American astronaut, 5'-4" tall, 117 lbs, married to Professor Matthew Duncan. Although lacking flight experience beyond Earth orbit, she was accepted as a member of the expedition upon the insistence of both Thompson and Duncan. Being a graduate nurse, with a degree in space medicine, she was a most valuable addition to the crew roster in her own right.

Valeri Karamov: 38-year-old Russian pilot, 5'-11" tall, 175 lbs, recently divorced and the father of a teen-age son. Among his achievements were two trips to the Moon, in which he acted as mission commander, and pilot of several shuttle flights to Space Station Prometheus. Thoroughly familiar with the operation of the mother ship, he was one of two astronauts scheduled to remain in orbit while his companions journeyed to the Martian surface.

Marina Selveg: 32-year-old Russian microbiologist/physician, 5'-4" tall, 120 lbs. A single brunette, her past achievements included a three-month stint in the main biological laboratory on Prometheus. She was reported to be an outstanding authority on long-term exposure to weak gravity, having recently published a highly acclaimed paper on the subject. Ever since the age of ten, when she had viewed Mars through a large telescope, she had wanted to visit the Red Planet.

Louis Alvarez: 36-year-old Spanish pilot, 6'-0" tall, some 206 lbs, married with two young daughters. During the course of his long career as an astronaut he had acquired a reputation of being one of the best shuttle pilots in the business, having made an impressive number of trips to ferry men and materials during the construction of the Mars Voyager. He was considered to be an able understudy for Thompson when it came to operating the landing module.

Brian Hawkins: 35-year-old English physicist, 5'-7" tall, 135 lbs, married with one son. Acknowledged to be an expert on their portable nuclear reactor, he was also somewhat of an electronics and computer wizard. While unable to boast of space travel beyond Prometheus, his skills were deemed essential for the success of the mission.

Frank Manzoni: 36-year-old Italian physicist, 6'-0" tall, 190 lbs, married with two small sons. Proficient in the workings of small nuclear reactors, he held degrees in both metallurgy and solid-state electronics. Totally lacking in previous space flight experience, he was accepted as a last minute replacement for Chou Lin, the Chinese contribution to the first Martian expedition some four years earlier. (Scheduled to be a member of the return team, Lin had been seriously injured in a hit-and-run motor accident.)

Sanjay Kanti: 38-year-old electrical engineer from Bombay, India, 5'-9" tall, 155 lbs, married with two teen-age daughters. Although lacking space travel experience beyond Prometheus, he had spent the best part of several years assembling components of both the Mars Voyager and Explorer spacecraft. By reason of his great technical expertise he was deemed to be a definite asset to the mission.

Carlos Niemeyer: 35-year-old Brazilian communications and computer specialist, 5'-8" tall, 145 lbs, married with one young daughter. His inclusion as a member of the expedition was almost a must in view of his extensive knowledge of electronics systems. Indeed, he had helped to supervise the installation of much of the more sophisticated equipment aboard both the mother ship and the smaller landing vehicle.

Henri Talon: 38-year-old French computer specialist, 5'-8" tall, 150 lbs. A confirmed bachelor and a veteran space traveler, with several excursions to the Moon to his credit, he was reported to be one of the brains behind a number of intricate systems that had been incorporated into the Mars Voyager. His talents would likely prove invaluable in deciphering the highly advanced alien technology.

Sato Tanaka: 35-year-old communications expert, 5'-8" tall, 155 lbs, married with one son. Noted for his expertise in the field of electronics, he had likewise assisted in the design and construction of the Mars Voyager. Along with Karamov, he was one of the two crew members designated to remain in orbit aboard the mother ship. Born in Japan, Tanaka was now an American citizen.

With an unprecedented number of TV viewers watching intently, the twelve astronauts exited the Prometheus in a shuttle craft. All cameras soon focused upon the glistening silver ship floating nearby. Renamed the "Celeste," it was the old Mars Voyager which had performed so well on its maiden flight. No longer the slim craft that had returned from the Red Planet, it had since been refurbished and now exhibited the same twin pods of solid fuel rockets with which it had departed on the initial venture.

Slung under the belly of the Celeste was a new landing craft identical to the first expedition's Explorer. For this return engagement the two-stage descent/ascent module was named the "Questor." As before, its cargo bay housed a portable nuclear reactor and a Rover tractor vehicle. A major difference was to be found in the much larger storage compartment of the Rover, which was fully twice the size of the original model. This was for the purpose of accommodating a second small reactor that would give them much needed electrical power inside the dark chambers of the alien "Face." Fortunately, this modification did not pose much of an engineering problem with regard to size or weight. No longer concerned with terrestrial exploration, considerably fewer storage batteries would be required. On the other hand, what did matter was the fact that the extra nuclear reactor would mean additional weight, thereby cutting into the fuel reserves of the Questor's descent stage.

Also to be considered, in conjunction with any weight problem, was the five new crew members. Not only would extra life support systems be required, but there was their consumable supplies for a surface stay of approximately one month. Other items contributing to a reduction of fuel reserves was the need to carry a quantity of lighting equipment, as well as an oxygen/acetylene cutting torch. Although the Selestian data sheets did tell of an internal lighting system that would automatically be activated upon opening the sealed green door, after an interval of some 300,000 years it was anything but a foregone conclusion that it would still work. Likewise, who was prepared to guarantee that the door would open after such a long period of time, even if the proper access code had been punched into the control panel? For this reason it had been decided to include the aforementioned equipment by way of insurance. There was certainly no point in coming all this way only to be frustrated at the last moment, just for the sake of a few simple items. It might be close, but it was finally agreed that this extra weight would still leave them with a small reserve of fuel for a safe landing - assuming, of course, that they did not encounter any unforeseen problems.

Over the span of the next four hours the Celeste's twelve crew members conducted a thorough check of many of the ship's complex systems. Not to be overlooked, the attached Questor was likewise subjected to scrutiny after the last of the maintenance workers had departed to Prometheus by return shuttle. Although nothing seemed to be amiss, there was always the fear that instruments could be made to give a false reading. Having already delayed their departure for one orbit about the Earth, in order to double check the functioning of one particular system, Thompson could no longer put off the inevitable and he gave the command to start the final countdown. If a concealed act of sabotage existed it was beyond his power to intervene.

With the historical day proclaimed a global holiday, by the governments of all participating nations, the eyes and ears of a large segment of the world's population were riveted to their TV screens. Upon the success of this mission lay the aspirations of Earth civilization. Never, in all the annals of recorded history, had so many people held such high hopes for the future. A new and glorious destiny awaited mankind, concealed within the Martian "Face" for these past 3,000 centuries. Its secrets were now made freely available to a society that could certainly use all of the help that it might find. While there had been some shocks and a great deal of controversy over the Selestian's philosophical and religious messages, there could be no doubt as to a willingness to accept all of the promised technological treasures.

Twin bursts of orange flame signaled ignition of the first pair of solid fuel rockets. Soon a second, third and fourth pair were ignited, on opposing wing pods. The big spacecraft began to accelerate its departure from Earth orbit. Telescopes on board Prometheus followed the flaming tails of fire for some minutes, until the rapidly dwindling image was eventually lost to sight as the orbiting space station passed behind an eclipsing Earth. By the time their cameras would again have an unobstructed view of the Celeste it would be long gone on its voyage to the Red Planet.

Spiraling outward from the Sun the Celeste continued to coast rapidly through space, having already acquired sufficient momentum to reach their destination in a little over three months. Until a scheduled mid-course correction there would be no need to initiate another rocket burn. When it did come time to make this delicate adjustment, some two months into the mission, it was with the twin liquid fuel rocket engines. Without this finely controlled burn they would almost certainly miss their target or, at least, enter into a most unsatisfactory orbit.

Shortly after successfully completing this important maneuver, Tanaka received a disturbing message from Earth. Although it was not entirely unexpected, since the Sun was currently in an active sunspot phase in its 11-year cycle, a gigantic solar flare had erupted and was spewing massive amounts of high energy protons and other forms of hard radiation in their direction. The full force of this intense storm was due to strike Earth within the next hour or so, when it would effectively disrupt all forms of radio and TV telemetry. An hour or two later dangerous levels were expected to reach the Celeste. Unless steps were taken to shield the crew they would likely be exposed to hazardous - possibly even lethal - amounts of radiation.

Sounding the alarm, Thompson fired the small jet thrusters which would change the orientation of the Celeste relative to the Sun. In anticipation of just such an occurrence, engineers had constructed heavy shielding around a forward compartment which served as a dual purpose lounge/dining room. By turning the ship so that the rear of the long cylindrical fuselage pointed toward the Sun, much of the radiation would be absorbed by fuel and water tanks. With radiation levels monitored by their instruments, it was felt that the solar flare would be more of an inconvenience than a serious threat. In the absence of this shielding it might well have proven a disaster.

"How long do you think it will last?" asked Manzoni, as he quite literally floated across the crowded compartment currently providing sanctuary.

"Impossible to say," answered Thompson. "Hopefully, it will only be a matter of hours before it subsides to more tolerable levels."

"What's the worst case scenario?" inquired Hawkins.

"Several days, I'm afraid," responded Karamov, resigned to the possibility of being couped up for some time.

"At least we aren't likely to go hungry," quipped the French computer expert. "The adjoining kitchen was wisely placed behind the shielding."

"Ditto for the lavatory," added Alvarez.

"How high a reading are we getting from the external sensors? Has it changed any during the past hour?" Marina wanted to know.

"Seems to be holding steady with only minor fluctuations," said Erica, peering intently at a computer print-out. "Had we been sitting on the outer hull we would have absorbed well over 600 rems by now - definitely a lethal dose."

"Did anyone think to bring a deck of playing cards?" asked Duncan.

Some twelve hours later a sharp drop in radiation levels was detected, and the crew of the Celeste began to breathe a sigh of relief. A check of their internal monitoring system revealed that the astronauts had absorbed close to ten rems, a not insignificant amount but still far below the safety threshold. Very shortly thereafter the radiation flux declined to an acceptable level and they felt free to at last leave the sanctuary of their temporary shelter. The experience had been a triumph over one of nature's threats. A lingering question, in the minds of certain members of the Celeste's crew, was whether the foolish actions of man would pose a greater danger.

The following week this nebulous fear became a very tangible reality after Tanaka received an urgent message from Earth. It was Mission Control asking for a person-to-person conversation with Thompson on a secure channel. Puzzled by the communication, Tanaka hastened to convey the unusual request. Ten minutes later the Celeste's commander was listening to the voice of Andrew L. Stanwick, chairman of Earth's second expedition to Mars. What he had to say was highly disturbing:

"The hit-and-run incident, which severely injured astronaut Chou Lin, was no ordinary accident, but a deliberate attempt to prevent him from participating in the mission. The individual involved in this crime was only recently apprehended. Although the local police were inclined to view the case as a simple hit-and-run affair, our investigators have since discovered that the culprit has strong ties with a fanatical religious group actively opposed to the Martian venture. Threatened with a lengthy prison term, upon promise of a reduced sentence he has now confessed to an insidious plot. While we have yet to unravel the details, it would appear that the only purpose for removing Lin was to make room for a saboteur substitute! Should this be so, then our chief suspect must logically be Frank Manzoni, his replacement. At the moment we are still trying to determine the full implications of this shocking development. Meanwhile, it is imperative to keep a watchful eye on Manzoni without arousing undue suspicion. Until we learn more, it is suggested that you use extreme caution when discussing this conversation with other crew members. Good luck to you all in your mission....Stanwick, over and out."

Acknowledging the message, Thompson unfastened his seat belt and launched himself across the room to the closed door of the communications compartment. Striking his target with more than a gentle thud, he proceeded to attach his adhesive shoes to the floor before opening the door which led into the adjoining lounge/ dining room. Spotting Tanaka sitting alone, sipping coffee from a closed container, he felt obliged to initiate conversation.

"I trust you didn't mention Mission Control's radio message to anyone else," he said to his communications specialist.

"No sir, I haven't said a word to any of the crew."

"Good! While I'm not at liberty to discuss matters at this very moment, I will say that it is definitely in the best interest of the mission to keep it a secret for now."

"You can count on me, Adam," said Tanaka. "Do you want me to erase Mission Control's request for a private conversation from the log tape?"

"I already have," Thompson replied, exiting the compartment.

Making his way to the pedestal which afforded access to the revolving wheel, he quickly climbed to the top of the hub, where he entered the spoke leading to the quarters shared by Professor Duncan and his wife. Reaching his destination, he pushed a door chime and was promptly ushered inside.

"You look worried, Adam," said Erica.

"I didn't realize it was that obvious."

"Never underestimate the perception of a woman with a degree in space medicine," remarked the professor.

"Please be seated and enjoy our artificial gravity, suggested Erica. "Would you care for some fruit juice that doesn't have to be consumed by means of a straw inserted into a sealed container?"

"Perhaps later, thank you. I'm afraid I have some disturbing news to tell you," Thompson said, wasting no time in getting right to the point of his visit.

"What is it?" asked Duncan, sensing that his close friend and colleague was truly upset over something.

Thompson proceeded to describe his recent conversation with Mission Control. He concluded with the need to keep this news secret from the rest of the crew, lest the saboteur be alerted. "You're the only ones that I know for certain who can be trusted," he said.

"It sure looks like Manzoni must be our man," conceded Duncan. "He's the sole member that was added to the crew roster after Chou Lin's injury."

"You know, Matt, it's almost inconceivable that one of us would be willing to sacrifice so much for the sake of heaven only knows what," lamented Thompson.

"Throughout history, both monetary gain and religious beliefs have always been strong motives," responded Erica.

"What form of sabotage are we most likely to be subjected to?" asked Duncan.

"If Manzoni had planed to sabotage the Celeste he could very easily have done so by now," Thompson stated.

"Which leaves the Questor. But how could he do serious damage to the landing module without sealing his own fate, since he is scheduled to go down to the surface?" Erica wanted to know.

"He couldn't," answered Thompson.

"Unless, of course, he is prepared to indulge in a suicide mission," said Duncan.

"Another possibility is that he might fake an excuse to remain aboard the Celeste," reasoned Erica.

"I'll make damn certain that he goes down to the surface!" exclaimed Thompson.

"An even better target than either the Celeste or the Questor might well be the alien artifacts themselves," Duncan suggested. "To destroy merely our spacecraft is to invite other expeditions."

"You're right, Matt, it would only postpone the inevitable," Thompson was forced to agree.

"The big question has got to be one of asking how the alien chambers could be destroyed. Could our portable nuclear reactor be converted into a low-yield atomic bomb?" asked Duncan.

"That's something I intend to find out right now. I'm going to have a discrete chat with Hawkins. He should know," Thompson said, rising to his feet.

"The very fact that Manzoni is a specialist in small nuclear reactors is perhaps rather ominous," Erica pointed out.

"I'll keep you informed of events," responded Thompson, as he moved swiftly toward the door.

It took him all of ten minutes to locate Hawkins at the rear of the catwalk between rows of storage tanks, where he was in the process of performing routine daily pressure checks. "Brian, may I have a word with you?" he asked.

"Of course. What's up?"

Feeling the need to confide in the expedition's only other nuclear reactor specialist, Thompson undertook to convey the gist of his conversation with Mission Control. He also told him of his discussion with Duncan and his wife.

"Am I to understand that just the four of us know about this sabotage threat?" uttered the visibly shaken physicist.

"Yes, and I would like to keep it that way for the present. My key question, Brian, is whether or not our portable reactor could be transformed into an atomic bomb."

"No, at least not as such," replied Hawkins. "To produce an atomic blast one has to bring a critical mass together rather quickly, by means of a special explosive device. There is no way in which our reactor could be adapted for this purpose."

"Thank heavens!" exclaimed Thompson.

"However, I have mentioned only one side of the coin," Hawkins was quick to add. "Total removal of the regulating rods would promptly cause the fission process to run wild, such as happened years ago at Three Mile Island and Chernobyl. Invariably, in a complete meltdown, massive amounts of highly radioactive debris would be released."

"How bad is the worst case scenario?"

"It could render the entire region of the inner chambers quite uninhabitable - possibly, for centuries!"

"Then that must be the plan. Tell me, is there any way to prevent the control rods from being withdrawn past the point of critical temperature?"

The physicist thought for a moment before answering: "There is a built-in safeguard for this very purpose. Unfortunately, it could be negated by one with the proper knowledge."

"Any suggestions?"

"Don't let Manzoni near the reactor without supervision."

"Then one of us will have to watch him at all times - unless, of course, I were to place him under arrest."

"Can you do that, on so little evidence?"

"I'll contact Mission Control and seek their advice on the matter," said Thompson. "Meanwhile, I'd appreciate it if you would keep this conversation to yourself. Should you see or hear anything even remotely suspicious, don't hesitate to let me know."

But as days turned into weeks, Stanwick had nothing further to add to his original warning. Thompson's orders remained the same. He was to watch carefully, but not to apprehend unless given some reason to do so.

The situation had not changed by the time the Celeste was inserted into Mars orbit. Igniting a series of their solid fuel rockets, they had first matched the velocity of the Red Planet's movement around the Sun. Several burns with their liquid fuel engines allowed them to enter into an elliptical orbit of the order of some eight hours and twelve minutes. Considering the planet's rotation period, this orbit would place them directly over the "Face" once every Martian day. Thus both a descent and ascent launch window would open up in just such an interval.

As before, Thompson found the view to be quite spectacular. For the others, it was a first time experience and a sight that they would never forget. The great rift valley complex of Valles Marineris stretched before them, as far as their eyes could see. Likewise, the Tharsis volcanoes were truly a scene to behold. At apogee, or high point of their orbit, the white polar caps were quite visible to the naked eye. At perigee, or point of closest approach, the "Face" could be seen clearly once every day through the ship's telescope. With no need for an extensive survey of the Martian landscape, their tourist holiday would not be a prolonged affair. Unless unforeseen circumstances intervened, they planned to depart for the surface in little more than forty hours. So far, everything had gone according to schedule and there was no hint of any suspicious act which would indicate sabotage.

Gathered together with the Duncans in the artificial gravity of their revolving wheel compartment, ostensibly for a game of bridge, were Thompson and Hawkins. The four were currently in the midst of a serious discussion of how to deal with the "Manzoni problem." To date, their chief suspect had given no clue as to his intended plan. Whatever he had in mind, neither the Celeste not the Questor appeared to be the target. While an examination of the portable reactor could be made before reaching the surface, they did know that it was untouched since departure from Earth orbit.

"The four of us will have to take turns watching Manzoni once we move the reactor inside the alien chamber," said Thompson. "We can't afford to leave him alone with it for a moment."

"How long would he need in order to start a runaway reaction?" asked Professor Duncan.

"I should say at least ten minutes," responded Hawkins. "Not only would he have to remove an elaborate housing, but a safeguard mechanism would need to be disassembled and a series of new wiring connections made."

"Assuming he does all this, exactly how much time would it take to initiate an actual meltdown?" asked Thompson.

"Probably less than a minute. I sure wouldn't want to stick around very long," Hawkins replied.

"What about a timing mechanism? Could it be rigged with such a device?" Erica wondered.

"He could probably connect an alarm clock or timer of some sort to the servo motor unit inside the reactor. Assuming that he had prepared the trigger beforehand, he could likely install it in another five to ten minutes," answered Hawkins.

"One question that must be resolved is the order of priority," said Thompson. "Since we would be spread much too thin to watch both Manzoni and the reactor, at all times, which should be given preference?"

"Perhaps we could alternate," suggested Erica. "This way any surveillance would be less conspicuous."

"On the other hand, watching only the reactor would allow us to guard against the possibility of there being another member of a conspiracy," said Duncan.

"Matt does have a point," declared Hawkins.

"Heaven forbid that there should be more than one saboteur in our midst!" exclaimed Thompson. "However, I do agree that our prime consideration should be the reactor, which we should monitor continuously."

"Is there anyone else whom we might trust among the landing party?" asked Erica. "It would certainly make our task easier if we could recruit another crew member."

"Good idea," said Duncan. "But it would be wise to exclude any candidate with strong religious ties or affinity for material wealth."

"Do we have any logical prospects?" asked Hawkins.

"I recently went through the dossiers of our colleagues with just this thought in mind," said Thompson. "Also, a few hours ago I received an updated report from Stanwick touching upon this very subject. It would seem that Kanti was raised as a Muslim; while Niemeyer is still considered to be a Catholic. Neither may be viewed as staunch adherents. Alvarez is evidently an ex-Catholic with his present religious affiliation, if any, unknown. Marina Selveg is described as merely the child of Catholic parents, with little apparent interest in the church herself. Only Talon can be said to be opposed to religious factions in general, having once written a college thesis denouncing orthodox religions in favor of an open mind. Also, he is reputed to have declined offers of much higher pay in industry so that he might pursue his career as an astronaut."

"Sounds like he could be our man," said Duncan.

"No objection from me," said Hawkins.

"Ditto," from Erica.

"Then it's agreed," responded Thompson. "I'll have a private chat with Talon at earliest convenience."

"Anything further on the hit-and-run driver that struck down Chou Lin?" asked Duncan.

"All they have been able to get out of him is that he was paid to do it by certain individuals they're still trying to apprehend. He says he was merely told that the elimination of Lin from the mission would greatly assist their cause. He recently passed a lie detector test with flying colors, so they believe he's telling the truth when he claims he doesn't know any more details," said Thompson.

"Shouldn't we inform Tanaka and Karamov before leaving the Celeste?" suggested Hawkins.

"I intend to do just that," declared Thompson.

Chapter 8

THE INNER CHAMBERS

Aboard the Questor all ten astronauts anxiously awaited the ignition of a single solid fuel rocket that would take them out of orbit and send them on their way to the Martian surface, which lay some 1,200 kilometers below. Numbers on a computer video screen were rapidly winding down to zero.

"Ignition!" shouted Thompson.

A sudden lurch coincided with the orange flame which spewed from the craft's descent stage. The Celeste appeared to recede and climb away at an increasing rate of speed and was soon lost to sight. Finally burning out, the rocket was promptly jettisoned as a measure to reduce weight. Aerobraking, thrust from their liquid fuel propulsion engines, and a drag-chute would subsequently be employed to slow their descent.

"We're entering the upper layers of the atmosphere," announced Thompson, as a feeling of weightlessness was soon interrupted by a noticeable shudder and a gentle push into the soft foam padding of their contoured seats.

"Trajectory looking good," voiced Alvarez, scanning the screen of the radar altimeter in front of him.

A steady pressure held them glued to their reclining seats; while an occasional burn with their liquid fuel engines subjected them to intervals of higher "G" force.

"Right on the mark," advised Alvarez...."Altitude approaching fourteen thousand meters."

At twelve thousand meters Thompson gave the order to deploy the drag-chute, which would help slow their still rapid rate of descent.

"Deploying chute," responded Alvarez, pushing the appropriate button. Nothing happened. Instead of a green light, signifying deployment, a red light showed on the instrument panel. "Damn!" he exclaimed, pushing the button again and again. "I've still got a red light!"

"It's definitely not activated," said Thompson. "You can feel a distinct jolt when it opens."

Thoughts of sabotage immediately came to the minds of at least five members of the crew. This was certainly not the worst thing that could go wrong. But would it be the last?

In order to compensate for the failed drag-chute, Thompson was compelled to initiate another rocket burn, lest they overshoot the target area by a considerable margin. Unfortunately, it would also erode their limited reserve of fuel. It now became a case of sacrificing proximity to the "Face" for the factor of safety. It would not be a wise decision to have no propellant left with which to avoid unforeseen obstacles at their landing site.

"Four percent fuel remaining," advised Alvarez....."Forward speed 105 meters per second....Altitude 1.4 kilometers....Rate of descent 14.5 meters per second."

Rotating the craft slightly, Thompson initiated a ten-second burn at 20% throttle. They were presently passing close to the "Face," which lay a scant 1.5 kilometers to the north.

"Two percent fuel....Altitude 250 meters....Forward speed 27.5 meters per second....Descent rate 4.5 meters per second," remarked Alvarez.

"Passing over some rough terrain," announced Erica, monitoring the video view from an outside camera.

Again rotating the craft, Thompson undertook to negate their descent speed so that forward momentum would carry them beyond the hazardous region. At last, having reached a reasonably flat area, he cancelled all lateral motion with another short rocket burn, allowing the Questor to sink straight down.

"Kicking up considerable dust," said Erica.

"Descent 1.2 meters per second....Altitude 10 meters...Forward speed zero," Alvarez called out.

With their twin rocket engines delivering a steady low-level thrust, the Questor settled gently to the ground on its shock absorber legs. Shutting down their propulsion system, they waited for the dust to settle, relieved at the thought that they had now arrived safely on the Martian surface - even if it was not quite as close to the "Face" as they would have liked. Just how close was determined shortly after visibility was restored and they were able to get an exact fix on their position.

"We appear to be at least ten kilometers from our target, in a straight line of sight," said Erica, upon comparing photos of the region with landmarks seen through their windows. "However, the path to our objective will be substantially greater, as there is an intervening section of rugged terrain."

Considering the drag-chute failure, all of the astronauts were unanimous in their praise of Thompson's skill in managing to land them safely and so near to the "Face." A check of their lower stage fuel reserve disclosed that less than one percent remained.

"We have a good eight hours of daylight left," said Thompson. "I suggest that we grab a quick bite to eat before exiting to the surface and setting up the Questor's reactor."

Within the span of the next two hours they were successful in accomplishing three key tasks. First, Niemeyer made contact with the Celeste and informed Tanaka of their safe landing, in spite of the drag-chute failure - a point upon which he elaborated to some extent. Second, the Questor's reactor was deployed and delivering a steady flow of electrical energy. Finally, they were able to remove the Rover from the cargo bay and ready it for a trip to the alien "Face."

A modified version of the initial Rover, used some four years earlier, it was built for storage capacity rather than cruising distance. Its more spacious rear compartment held a second and fully portable nuclear reactor. It also contained a quantity of floodlights with which to illuminate the dark interior of the Selestian complex. Yet another item, lacking on mankind's first expedition, was an oxygen/acetylene cutting torch - in case the mysterious green door would not respond to decoded instructions. Five crew members (Thompson, Duncan, Hawkins, Manzoni, Alvarez) were all that could be accommodated on this initial trip.

Amidst a chorus of encouraging cheers and high expectations they departed with Thompson at the controls.

"We're video taping your departure," announced Niemeyer, over their radio link.

"This sure brings back old memories," said Thompson, swerving to circumvent a cluster of large boulders.

"At least we're within walking distance if we should suffer a breakdown," remarked Alvarez.

"An explorer must always be an optimist," Thompson was prompt to philosophize. "Say, one day, when we have more time, it would be interesting to see if a path could be found for the Rover to negotiate a more direct route through this obstacle maze. As it is, a safe roundabout course will probably double the distance to our objective." (At this point in time there was no way to know that failure of the drag-chute, combined with this annoying patch of rough terrain, would later prove to be a blessing in disguise.)

It took them approximately forty minutes to reach the vicinity of the "Face." From a distance of a few hundred meters it looked quite similar to other mesa protrusions on the Martian surface. Approaching the "chin," one could see a small silvery area which glistened in the bright sunshine.

"There it is, folks," Thompson stated, pointing to the alien door. "You are now beholding the lid to Pandora's box."

"I only hope the world will appreciate the precious legacy that the Selestians have seen fit to bestow upon us," commented Duncan.

Clad in their protective space suits, four adventurers exited from the cramped confinement of the Rover's small air lock. Only Hawkins remained on board in order to drive the vehicle inside the alien chamber once the outer door had been opened.

"With all their advanced technology you'd think they would have installed an automatic door opener," complained Manzoni.

Noting that only a small amount of sand had drifted around the entrance during the past four years, Thompson activated the lever which would give them access.

"Do you think we should try the kick technique or the proven stampede charge to gain entry?" quipped Duncan.

"Hopefully, neither method will be necessary," said Thompson, giving the door a firm push.

To the delight of all it opened without requiring any drastic measures, revealing the same pitch black interior that had so frustrated Chadwick and Thompson during the first expedition to the Red Planet. Moments later Hawkins drove the Rover into the alien's outer chamber, its headlights serving to cast shifting shadows on the walls and arched ceiling. At the far end of the cavern could be seen the closed green door, the object of their mission.

"Park it over by the inner door," requested Thompson, over his helmet radio link.

"Read you loud and clear," answered Hawkins, as he brought the Rover to a stop about ten meters away from the Selestian air lock.

Wasting little time they unloaded their portable reactor and moved it to a safe distance, thankful for the wheels which allowed it to roll freely on the hard, non-skid surface of the floor. It was not long before a series of floodlights illuminated the entire chamber. While one group examined and video taped the scenery, a second was concerned with the task of opening the green door. In the event that the alien locking mechanism should fail to respond to command, after an estimated 300,000 years, there was always the cutting torch which had been placed beside the metallic door.

"According to the data sheets all seven push buttons have to be activated in sequence," said Duncan. "What I propose to do is to inscribe each button with our own system of numerals, so that all we have to do is push buttons numbered from one to seven."

"Sounds like a good idea," agreed Thompson.

Taking a notebook from a pocket of his suit, Duncan began to convert the Selestian symbols to figures they could understand. "There, this should give us the proper order," he declared, upon affixing a series of numerical labels to the push buttons. "Who wants to try it out?"

"Be my guest," said Thompson. "You're the one who decoded these hieroglyphics."

Duncan pushed the prescribed sequence of buttons. They waited for something to happen. To their astonishment, just when they were beginning to think in terms of resorting to a cutting torch, all pandemonium seemed to break loose. The entire outer chamber burst into brilliance, as sections of the walls and ceiling began to glow from a light source evidently incorporated into their very structure. Simultaneously, the green door swung open of its own accord, disclosing a spacious illuminated air lock with a large blue door at the opposite end. But what really startled them was a loud shrieking sound which came over their suit radios. Lasting for a full seven seconds, it ceased as abruptly as it had begun.

"What the devil was that?" shouted Alvarez, amidst a chorus of voices expressing similar comments over their radio link.

"Would anybody care to subscribe to an alien burglar alarm theory?" asked Hawkins.

"Unless I'm mistaken, the very act of opening the air lock door has just triggered a message to the Galactic Society. I do believe it has notified them that Earth has now developed a space-faring civilization," opined Duncan. "Although it is not widely known, in the data sheets the Selestians did mention that a signal would go out once the inner chamber was breached."

"Does this mean that we can expect a visit from an alien spaceship in the foreseeable future?" Thompson asked.

"I would venture to say sometime before the end of the present millennium," Duncan answered.

"I only hope that mankind is ready for them," said Hawkins.

"So do I," agreed Duncan.

"Let's try out the air lock," suggested Thompson.

Entering the airless chamber, the five explorers closed the green door behind them and approached the blue door. Noting that it displayed the same sequence of push button inscriptions, Duncan proceeded to mark the buttons as before. Upon activation, they were promptly rewarded by a rush of air into the chamber. Within a few minutes the flow of air ceased and the blue door swung open to expose a brightly illuminated interior.

"Can we trust that the air is safe to breathe?" Manzoni wanted to know.

"I would think so," replied Duncan. "The Selestian's home planet is described as being very similar to Earth. Also, they are supposed to have sterilized the interior, so that no trace of potentially dangerous microbes would be left."

"Air pressure and oxygen/nitrogen ratio appear to be quite acceptable," announced Thompson, after studying the dials of a test instrument which he held.

"Any reward for volunteering to be the first human guinea pig?" asked Hawkins, removing his helmet.

Observing no ill effects, one by one the others shed their cumbersome space suits. The air seemed fresh and invigorating, with perhaps a slight hint of antiseptic quality. There was no question but what the "Face" would be of immense value when it came time for mankind to colonize Mars.

Anxious to explore what was evidently a labyrinth of chambers and passageways, Thompson chose to keep the group together. Until they became more familiar with the layout it would be very easy to get lost. The last thing he wanted was to waste time in a search for missing colleagues. Besides, he needed to keep a watchful eye on Manzoni at all times.

Fortunately, the Selestians proved to be considerate absentee hosts. Not far from the entrance air lock they came across what was clearly a map of the alien complex. It was incorporated into the wall at the junction of several corridors.

"Just like a directory at a large indoor shopping mall," said Alvarez, examining the graphics closely.

"I think it might be prudent to make a copy of this map," suggested Duncan. "Not only could it save us from retracing our steps or getting lost, but if I can decode these symbols it should allow us to visit areas of greatest interest."

"Good idea," said Thompson. "Let's take the time to study the floor plan of this veritable maze before proceeding any further."

Some ten minutes later Duncan had drawn a reasonably accurate map which depicted a number of chambers that warranted attention. Several others were described by symbols which would require some time to decipher. One of the decoded areas, which lay close to their present location, was a cluster of rooms designated as being living quarters. For the sake of convenience they decided to give it first priority.

Entering one of the chambers, they were visibly impressed with the state of preservation. The furniture seemed to be made out of a strange type of plastic. It was both durable and strong, while soft to the touch. It also came in a variety of pleasing colors. Even the material on the bed had not deteriorated after a period estimated to be of the order of 300,000 years! Without a doubt, they must take a sample of this strange substance back to Earth for detailed analysis. However, their greatest surprise came when they investigated the kitchen and bathroom. They actually had running water - even hot water - at their disposal!

"Most incredible!" exclaimed Manzoni. "Now I can take a real shower. I haven't had one in months."

"I know!" said Hawkins, under his breath.

The kitchen held a number of sophisticated electronic devices, the functions of which completely eluded them. "It might be well not to play with any of the controls until we know what we are doing," advised Thompson.

Receiving no argument on this point, the group moved into what was thought to be a combination living/family/study room. Like the kitchen, it possessed a variety of unfamiliar gadgets which aroused their curiosity.

"I believe that I recognize some of these inscriptions without recourse to my notebook," declared Duncan. "This is a symbol for an on/off switch; while this word relates to noise level. It must control either a video screen or our equivalent of a CD player."

"Seems harmless enough," said Thompson. "Why not give it a try? As long as it has an off button we can't do much damage."

"It probably doesn't work after all these years," remarked Alvarez, expressing a degree of pessimism.

Duncan pushed a button. To their astonishment, an entire wall lit up and projected a 3-D image that was extremely realistic with regard to both color and clarity. The scene was of a picturesque lake surrounded by a profusion of colorful vegetation. A soft and melodious sound could be heard in the distance.

"I think this has something to do with switching channels," said Duncan, pushing another button.

The wall scene promptly shifted to what appeared to be moving ocean waves washing upon some beach, complete with appropriate sound effects. A beautiful sunset constituted the background.

"I would have to say that we are viewing a Selestian wall mural," concluded Duncan, as he proceeded to change channels. In due succession, a total of twelve different scenes were projected before it recycled to the original view.

"This is certainly much better than hanging a painting on the wall," declared Hawkins. "My wife would surely go crazy with one of these devices."

As they were about to vacate the apartment a small object caught Thompson's eye. "I wonder what this is?" he asked, picking it up.

It was a cube, approximately 12 cm to a side, with several tiny buttons and a dial of some sort. It also had a recessed square at the center of one of its faces. A small hole could be seen in the middle of the side which evidently constituted the top. Extending from the cube to a nearby wall receptacle was a thin insulated cord. Close by lay a number of much smaller cubes, each about 12 mm across.

Recognizing the by now familiar markings signifying an on/off button, Thompson gave it a push. Nothing happened. Conceding that it no longer worked, he set it down without turning it off.

"Probably a broken toy," suggested Hawkins.

"These little cubes seem designed to fit inside the recess of the larger cube," said Duncan, picking up one at random. To prove his point he inserted it into the depression. Almost immediately he jumped back in surprise. From the tiny hole at the top of the cube a holographic image was projected into the room. About one cubic meter in size, it depicted one of the alien's great spaceships in full color and with perfect clarity.

"I wonder what this dial does?" remarked Hawkins, giving it a twist. The image promptly increased in size until it reached a maximum of three meters to a side - almost the exact height of the ceiling.

"Some toy!" voiced Thompson. "I'm anxious to see what near miracles their real treasures can perform."

Curious to find out what would happen if he severed the wall connection, Duncan reached over and gave it a gentle tug, popping the plug out of the receptacle. His action failed to affect the holograph in any way. "Must be using a rechargeable battery as an energy source," he deduced.

"Let's try another button," said Thompson, moving toward the intriguing alien device.

Each time they activated the button a different image was caused to appear. After a dozen or so holographs it was decided to defer further experimentation in favor of more urgent matters. Turning the machine off, Thompson reconnected the power cord to the wall plug and led the group to an adjoining apartment. For all intents and purposes, it was virtually identical with the one they had just explored.

"According to our directory map there are at least a dozen family apartments in this particular complex," announced Duncan.

"We still have a good three hours of daylight remaining," said Thompson, glancing at his wrist watch. "I see no reason why we shouldn't pick up the rest of the crew from the Questor. I'm sure they would appreciate the luxurious accommodation the aliens have left for us."

"I could go back for them, if you wish," Hawkins volunteered.

"Thanks, Brian, but I think I should go myself. There are a number of things that I want to do," replied Thompson. "Why don't the rest of you guys select your own rent-free apartment?"

With an offer that could not be refused, after some months of living in cramped quarters, there was soon a mad stampede toward a nearby exit from the room.

"Oh, Matt, could I see you for a moment?" Thompson asked, as Duncan was about to leave.

"Of course. What's up, Adam?"

Checking to make certain that the others had left, Thompson handed his companion an automatic pistol. "It carries a clip of twelve shells," he said. "Keep an eye on our friend Manzoni while I'm gone."

"I didn't realize that we had any firearms on the expedition."

"Mission Control called me aside just before we departed. In view of the sabotage threat they decided to slip me the gun as a safeguard. Please try to keep it a secret."

"It's safe with me," responded Duncan, concealing the weapon in a jacket pocket.

Making his way to the air lock Thompson quickly suited up and cycled through to the outer chamber. In a few minutes the Rover was churning across the Martian landscape on the way back to the Questor. Establishing radio contact en route, he endeavored to describe their discoveries and told his audience of his plan to transport the entire crew to the "Face."

Upon arrival, Thompson proffered a list of supplies that they would need for an extended stay inside the alien complex. Chief among these requirements would be food and drinking water. Until Dr. Selveg could analyze the Selestian water supply, and declare it to be free of harmful organisms, they would not take such an unnecessary risk.

"Unless we stumble upon a gourmet restaurant, I'm afraid we'll have to subsist on our usual diet of dehydrated delicacies," said Thompson.

"Just when I had hopes of dining in a Selestian luxury hotel," Talon remarked.

"I've got Tanaka on screen, Adam. He wants to congratulate you in person, so to speak," Niemeyer informed him.

Following a brief conversation with his communication expert aboard the Celeste, Thompson undertook to transmit contents of the day's video taping. He could imagine the excitement back on Earth when scenes of the inner chambers were broadcast to billions of intrigued viewers.

Within the span of the next hour they had managed to load the prescribed supplies aboard the Rover and were on their way to the Martian "Face." The journey itself proved both fascinating and uneventful, and it was not long before Thompson brought the yellow tractor to a stop close to the green door.

"End of the line and everybody out," said Thompson, reaching for the helmet to his pressure suit.

"I was kind of hoping that we could take the grand tour around the perimeter of the alien structure," voiced Kanti, more in jest than in actual disappointment.

"Some other occasion, perhaps, when we have more time and more daylight," responded Thompson.

"I can visualize tourists of the future paying a fortune to see the sights that we have seen," Talon remarked.

"What I would really like to do is climb up the stairway to the top," said Erica.

"But only after removing a certain boulder," added Marina. "I have never fancied myself as a mountain climber."

Exiting the Rover's air lock, Thompson closed the outer door of the alien complex and then proceeded to hook up a power supply cord from their portable reactor to the vehicle's battery system. "It always pays to have fully charged batteries," he explained.

With passengers and supplies placed inside the alien air lock, Thompson decided to try an experiment. Instead of closing the green door, he immediately punched in the code to open the blue door, wondering what would happen. To his satisfaction, no air began to rush into the air lock. The green door, however, closed of its own accord. Only then did air begin to flood the chamber. This was just as well, he thought, since it would otherwise be possible for one exiting the air lock to inadvertently (or even on purpose!) fail to close the outer door - thereby preventing others from cycling through.

In a short while the air pressure was equalized and the blue door automatically swung open. Lugging equipment and supplies, they stepped across the threshold into a realm which featured the advanced technology of the Selestians.

"All guests kindly remove their space suits when entering the Hilton Face, which comes complete with running water," announced Thompson. "Please place them in an orderly row to the right of the blue door."

First to greet the new arrivals was Hawkins. "You will be delighted to learn that Matt has figured out how to operate the alien's equivalent of a microwave oven. I trust you thought of bringing more food," he added.

"Not to worry. Ten servings of heated dehydrated food coming up, just as soon as you show me the kitchen," Erica assured the hungry physicist.

One hour later she was true to her word, as all ten explorers were gathered together in what now passed for a communal dining room.

"It took a little experimenting before we were able to get it down to a science," confessed Erica, responding to compliments. "Their version of a microwave is approximately ten times faster than ours. Also, they neglected to provide a cookbook informing us of this minor detail."

"Say, is it my imagination or is the light getting dimmer?" Alvarez questioned.

"I do believe he's right. It is noticeably darker," agreed Kanti.

Rising from his seat Duncan moved to the doorway which led out of the apartment. "It's also gotten darker outside. Unless I'm mistaken, their lighting system must be linked to the Martian cycle of night and day," he theorized.

"Does this mean that we'll have to resort to candles?" asked

Niemeyer.

Noting a small protruding wheel mechanism on a nearby wall, Duncan gave it a slight twist. The room darkened considerably. Reversing direction, the room brightened to its former level. "A simple rheostat," he declared.

With their appetites appeased, Thompson proceeded to discuss plans for the following day. In order to expedite matters they would be divided into two groups of five explorers. Thompson's group would include Duncan, Erica, Hawkins and Manzoni. Talon would lead the other group comprised of the remaining members. Each group would carry a map of the complex. In addition, each member would be supplied with their own personal walkie-talkie radio tuned to a common channel.

"I guess I may as well hand out the communicators now," said Thompson, reaching for a nylon bag at his side.

"How is the reception in here? Have you tried them out yet?" inquired Kanti.

"They seem to work fine in the limited area that we have tested," said Duncan. "We'll know tomorrow whether this holds throughout the entire system of passageways."

"You will note that our selected frequency is channel 10," said Thompson, handing out the last of the radios.

"What time do we start our exploration?" asked Alvarez.

"Let's make it 08 hours, by our time," replied Thompson. "It will be Martian daylight by then and all the lights in the complex should be on."

Dismissed, the congregation split up and began to file out of the room. By previous arrangement, the Duncans, Hawkins and Talon remained with Thompson after the others had left.

"Before leaving the Celeste I had Tanaka modify five of our radios," confided Thompson. "Only the buzzer on our instruments is activated by channel 44, which is the one that we will use to communicate with each other without Manzoni knowing."

"Sounds like a good idea," said Talon. "Have you devised a monitoring program?"

"I propose putting the air lock on constant surveillance, since nobody could tamper with the reactor without first passing through the air lock," replied Thompson. "We'll take two hour shifts, starting as soon as possible. Any objection to adopting the following order: Erica, Matt, Brian, Henri and myself?"

With all four of his colleagues in agreement, Thompson felt confident that the situation was well in hand. He looked forward to an exciting day of discovery come morning.

As it turned out, the night passed quite uneventful and with no indication that anything was amiss. At the prescribed hour all ten adventurers gathered together and set out on their mission of exploration. Talon and his group would investigate a cluster of adjoining compartments that were described as a science/medical center; while Thompson's team would check out what Duncan believed was the power source for the Selestian complex. According to the alien wall directory, they were located in opposite corners at the end of the "Face's" rectangular layout. At the very center of the entire structure was what appeared to be a courtyard. They would remain together in one group until reaching this junction.

"This is truly an amazing engineering achievement," remarked Kanti. "There must be nearly a hundred rooms and chambers, to say nothing of dozens of passageways."

"Without a map one could easily get lost in here," announced Marina. "By the way, Adam, I performed several tests on the alien water supply last night. So far everything looks fine. I'll let you know for certain by tomorrow."

"Speaking of water, I think I hear what sounds like a fountain or waterfall," declared Erica.

Sure enough, as they rounded a corridor they came to what was clearly the central courtyard. In its midst they beheld a large fountain discharging a considerable volume of water. Overflowing its walls in miniature cataracts, the water streamed into three ponds that were connected by winding channels. They stopped and gazed upon the scene in awe.

"So much for the dry planet theory!" exclaimed Talon.

"There's no way this thing could have been flowing for 300,000 years," opined Niemeyer.

"I rather suspect that it has lain dormant for all this time," suggested Duncan. "Like the lighting system, it was most likely programmed to come on when we triggered some mechanism by opening the green door."

"They probably grew a variety of vegetation in sections of the courtyard," theorized Hawkins, noting extensive areas of what was presumed to be sterile Martian soil. To support this premise he pointed to the high arched ceiling, from which hung suspended an exceptionally bright globe - fulfilling very nicely the function of an artificial sun.

"This place must have been a veritable paradise when in its prime," said Marina. "I can just visualize people strolling down Main Street to the park."

"Why would they ever want to leave after putting so much labor into constructing this place?" Alvarez asked.

"The Selestians evidently considered it a moral duty to spread their philosophy and culture to other emerging civilizations," said Duncan. "They have certainly left us a legacy totally beyond price. I only pray that we will prove worthy of it."

More than one member of the group cast a surreptitious glance at Manzoni, eager to glimpse any change of facial expression at this mention of spreading an alien philosophy. More than one of them thought that it had indeed struck a nerve.

With thoughts of Duncan's words still in mind, Thompson said: "I guess this is where we split up to go our separate ways. We'll communicate with each other every hour on the hour."

Passing several areas which they decided to mark for future study, Thompson led his party to what was believed to be the main alien power source. A large metallic door barred their entrance into the chamber. Half expecting it to be locked, Hawkins turned a lever. It opened without effort, exposing a strange spherical device which was estimated to be about three meters in diameter. It sat squarely in the middle of a spacious room, and was totally encased by a harmless looking wire fence.

"It appears to be constructed of an alloy similar to the door - possibly, an alloy including titanium and stainless steel," said Manzoni, referring to the fence.

"Whatever its purpose, I have to suspect that they don't want anyone to interfere with what's inside," reasoned Hawkins.

"Can you decode these inscriptions, Matt?" asked Thompson, as he drew attention to some rather bold markings on a nearby wall - markings which seemed especially designed to catch their eye.

Taking out his pocket dictionary of the Selestian language (a copy of which was possessed by all members of the landing party), Duncan began the task of deciphering the alien text. "You're not going to like what it says," he announced, after a few minutes had elapsed.

"Does it say to keep out?" guessed Thompson.

"Words to that effect, I'm afraid," said Duncan. "It tells us that the device is a matter/antimatter reactor, and that it will shut down automatically if disturbed in any way."

"You mean it could plunge us into total darkness?" questioned Erica.

"Exactly!" responded her husband.

"Then we certainly don't want to disturb it," said Thompson.

"There's more," continued Duncan. "Such a reactor constitutes the power source of their great starships - a secret which they do not want us to know at our present state of development. Also, they say that any tampering with the reactor will cause certain vital components to self-destruct, thereby assuring that no useful information will be obtained."

"Well, so much for this compartment," said Thompson. "I would suggest that we finish video taping any other inscriptions we come across and resume our exploring elsewhere."

Noticing somewhat smaller Selestian text on another wall, both Hawkins and Manzoni proceeded to record the ancient symbols for later study. Duncan, who had gone over to the inscriptions and was already at work with his translation, was heard to remark: "It appears to be some technical data listing the power output of the reactor as a function of what I interpret as being background flux radiation."

"Conceivably, our physicists will want to take a look at such details later," said Thompson, deferring the matter. "Let's see what treasures the other compartments hold."

By the time both groups had returned to their luxurious rent-free quarters it was very nearly the end of Martian daylight and they were famished. Following their communal dinner of heated reconstituted turkey, sweet potatoes and broccoli, they exchanged news of their respective searches. Talon's group, it was found, had been the more productive.

"We discovered two of the machines which are reputed to cure cancer," Dr. Selveg told them. "It's not a small device, weighing perhaps two or three hundred kilograms in terms of Earth gravity. However, it does come apart in three sections, according to what we learned from deciphering associated text."

"Did they furnish plans for its construction?" asked Thompson.

"So far, all we've been able to find is what appears to be operating instructions. We think they intended for us to take the apparatus back for analysis - very possibly, because the actual technology would be so difficult to translate," elaborated the petite Russian physician/microbiologist.

"We'll certainly plan to take one of the machines back with us," said Thompson. "If it works as well as they claim, it will be a prize to end all prizes."

"We also came across what we believe is the promised elixir that extends the life span of biological entities," Talon informed the group.

"What is it, carrot juice?" quipped Manzoni.

"Actually, it's a type of one-a-day pill. Inasmuch as they elected to supply both samples and a detailed map describing the molecular structure of the compound, there should be no problem in synthesizing it in the laboratory," explained Dr. Selveg.

"Great! When can I start taking them?" asked Hawkins.

"The line forms on the left," said Erica.

"This makes item number two on our list of treasures to bring back," stated Thompson. "Anything else to report?"

"We think we've found the apparatus that is supposed to give us unlimited amounts of clean, cheap electricity," said Kanti. "It appears to be a fusion reactor capable of converting heavy hydrogen into helium - something our scientists have been working on in vain for many years."

"Which compartment is it in? I'll have our physicists give it a close look first thing in the morning," responded Thompson, as he reached for his map of the alien complex.

"It was thought best to leave it undisturbed until it could be examined by more qualified experts," said Talon, proceeding to identify the compartment in question.

Agreeing that it had been a most productive day, in spite of their frustration with the matter/antimatter reactor, it was soon decided to conclude the meeting and let everyone take a deserved rest. Tomorrow would be another busy day. As before, the five members of the "Manzoni watch" committee remained behind after the others had left.

"Same order of monitoring the air lock tonight acceptable to all?" Thompson asked.

With no objections voiced, the group quickly dispersed, each to their own luxurious apartment suite.

Hours later, Thompson was awakened from a deep sleep by a loud pounding on the door to his quarters. "Who is it?" he asked.

"It's me, Hawkins."

"Come in, Brian. What time is it?"

"Almost time for you to relieve Henri," said Hawkins, entering and closing the door behind him. "I'm afraid I have some rather disturbing news to tell you."

"What news?"

"After my shift I couldn't get back to sleep, so I had a crack at decoding the text that I had taped inside the matter/antimatter reactor room. Unless I'm badly mistaken, there's potential for a disaster of the highest magnitude."

"How's that?"

"You will recall that Matt was saying the alien inscriptions had something to do with power output in terms of the flux of any background radiation," Hawkins began.

"Yes, I remember. Go on."

"Well, upon deciphering further, I discovered that a higher background flux leads to a marked increase in output - one that rises most alarmingly once a critical threshold is reached."

"How alarmingly?"

"If exposed to a sudden release of intense radiation, such as would occur if our portable reactor were to melt down, in a brief instant it could blow this place apart with at least the force of a powerful hydrogen bomb!"

Visibly shaken, Thompson began to dress with the utmost haste.

"Do you think Manzoni might have figured this out?" he asked.

"He certainly has the means and ability to do so."

"Damn! At first light, about an hour from now, I'm going to take our reactor and dump it in some obscure Martian crater," said Thompson, picking up his pistol and concealing it inside a jacket pocket.

In an instant the two were on a dead run toward the alien air lock. Reaching it, they looked around in vain for Talon, who was supposed to be watching the exit. There was nobody to be seen.

"We'd better check and make certain that our reactor is still safe and sound in the outer chamber," voiced Thompson, picking up a space suit.

Ten minutes later both Thompson and Hawkins had cycled through the green door. A short distance away the Rover stood where it had been parked. Their portable nuclear reactor, however, was conspicuous by its absence! Also missing was the oxyacetylene torch, which had been left standing nearby.

Chapter 9

VISIT TO PHOBOS

Alarmed by theft of the reactor, Thompson and his companion promptly cycled back through the air lock. With this sudden turn of events, they had to face the fact that Talon must have been overpowered before he could call for help - unless, of course, he was one of the conspirators himself! The thought of this second possibility was highly disconcerting, to say the least.

Activating surveillance channel 44 on his radio, Thompson made an urgent call to Duncan and informed him of events. "Hawkins and I are going straight to the matter/antimatter chamber," he said. "We think Manzoni may be headed there with our reactor. Notify the others and let me know who is missing."

"Will do," responded Duncan, who had just been aroused from a sound sleep by the incessant buzzing of his communicator.

"What is it?" asked Erica, now fully awake beside her husband.

"Thompson and Hawkins have just discovered Talon missing and our portable reactor gone. Adam wants us to alert the others and check to see who is absent from their room."

A few minutes later Erica had apprised Marina of the shocking development; while Duncan had managed to roust both Niemeyer and Kanti. As expected, Manzoni's apartment was vacant and he was not to be found. Continuing down the corridor they came to Talon's quarters, which was also empty. The last one on their list to be checked was Alvarez, whom they found wide awake and experimenting with one of the small holographic cubes that had proved to be so fascinating.

"We suspect that Manzoni has stolen our portable reactor and is planning to blow up the complex by causing a meltdown inside the matter/antimatter chamber," Duncan told him.

"What!"

Repeating himself, and adding news of Talon's disappearance, Duncan found him more than willing to assist in locating the vital reactor and their two missing colleagues. Leaving the two girls to watch the air lock, he had the others spread out in a hasty room-to-room search.

Meanwhile, Hawkins and Thompson had just reached the Selestian reactor compartment. To their utter horror, the metal door to the chamber was welded shut and the hoses to the oxyacelyene torch had been completely severed. Moreover, the contents of the tanks were already dissipated through valves that had been left wide open - eliminating any possibility of using the equipment to cut their way in. Of Manzoni or the reactor there was no trace. They had little doubt as to where the reactor might be found. In truth, the fate of the Martian "Face" seemed as good as sealed!

"How much time do you think we've got?" asked Hawkins, still endeavoring to recover from the great shock.

"Unless he intends to commit suicide, he would have to time it so that the Questor could intercept the Celeste," Thompson pointed out.

"When is the next launch window?"

"In about two hours," Thompson answered, reaching for his radio communicator.

However, before he could speak a word the buzzer sounded to inform him that a call was coming through on channel 10. It was Alvarez, reporting that he had spotted Manzoni moving toward the fusion reactor, located deep inside the complex. Ascertaining that Duncan was the closest member of the search team, Thompson dispatched him to investigate. Kanti, Niemeyer and Hawkins were sent to join the girls at the air lock; while he himself would leave to assist Duncan and Alvarez in the chase.

Moments later Kanti radioed to say that he had found Talon, unconscious and badly injured, concealed in a washroom in one of the unused apartments not far from the air lock. With the arrival of Niemeyer at the exit, Dr. Selveg and Erica hastened to tend to their wounded companion.

"Looks like he was struck over the head with a blunt weapon of some sort," remarked Kanti, as Marina bent down to examine Talon.

"I'm afraid it's very serious," she said, presently. "He's barely clinging to life with a severely fractured skull."

"I'd better join Niemeyer at the air lock," said Kanti, as he exited the apartment.

The scene which greeted Kanti, as he reached his destination, was one of considerable shock. Niemeyer was doing his best to defend himself against Manzoni and Alvarez, with his communicator laying smashed on the floor. Immediately after radioing Thompson for help, he witnessed Manzoni stab Niemeyer in the chest with a knife. Entering the fray, he could only hope to delay any escape through the air lock until assistance arrived.

With Thompson and Duncan setting out for the battle scene on the dead run, Hawkins was the next to reach the air lock. Both Niemeyer and Kanti lay dying on the floor, while two space-suited figures were observed in the act of slitting the remaining suits. He grabbed one of them from behind and threw him to the ground. The other saboteur promptly diverted his attention to the rather diminutive physicist, brandishing a wicked looking blade. Deftly sidestepping a thrust, Hawkins delivered an accurate kick which sent his adversary sprawling. Unfortunately, his first opponent had recovered and was likewise in possession of a knife. The odds were definitely not in his favor, and it was not long before one of them caught him with a slash to his shoulder.

Just when all appeared lost, help arrived on the scene in the form of Thompson and Duncan. The two villains made a dash for the open air lock. Pistol in hand, Thompson immediately fired. One of the figures staggered and fell; while the other escaped through the air lock, closing the door behind him. Upon reaching the door Thompson quickly punched in the proper code. But he was too late; the exit code had already been entered at the green door. Until the occupant had departed the chamber there was no way that it could be made to recycle.

"Damn!" exclaimed Thompson. "By the time we can get through to the outer chamber he'll be long gone in the Rover."

Radioing for medical assistance, Duncan attempted to staunch the flow of blood from Hawkins' shoulder. He did not have long to wait as both girls soon made their appearance, having heard the cry for help over their communicators.

"Get me the first aid kit, Erica, while I take over," Marina said, relieving Duncan of duty.

"They've ripped four of them to pieces," said Thompson, after examining the pile of crumpled pressure suits lying on the floor.

"How about the others?" Duncan asked.

"They seem to be untouched," replied Thompson, already in the process of slipping into one of the undamaged suits. "They were interrupted in the nick of time."

Removing the helmet of the shot saboteur, Duncan announced: "It's Manzoni, and he's still conscious."

"Why?" asked Marina. "Why did you ever want to destroy such a priceless legacy?"

"They....they denied the existence of our Lord Jesus Christ," stammered Manzoni, coughing up a quantity of blood from his chest wound.

"I fear there are none so blind as those who won't see; nor as fanatical as one committing a vile act of terrorism in the name of religion." lamented Duncan.

"When is it set to explode?" Hawkins wanted to know.

"In about three hours," whispered Manzoni. "I'm sorry....It was nothing personal....you understand." He gave one last gasp and fell silent.

"Incidentally, Talon passed away just before you radioed for help," said the physician.

"Quick, Matt, get into one of these suits," Thompson urged. "If we can't catch Alvarez before he reaches the Questor we're as good as doomed."

Duncan hastened to comply.

"How can you ever hope to outrun the Rover - especially since he's got such a head start?" asked Erica, arriving with Marina's medical kit.

"We do have a chance. Alvarez must take a rather circuitous route in order to avoid obstacles. On the other hand, we can run fast in the reduced Martian gravity and take a short cut across rough terrain," explained Thompson.

"I only hope we can find our way through the maze of boulders and craters without getting lost or breaking our necks," remarked Duncan.

"So do I," said Thompson.

Noting that there were just four good space suits, and five crew members in need of one, Erica began to remove Manzoni's suit. "A small bullet hole should not pose too much of a problem, if our repair patches work as well as they claim," she said.

"As soon as you can, I want the three of you to suit up and follow us out the air lock," directed Thompson. "Take the path made by the Rover's tracks. If we're successful in stopping him we'll come back that way and pick you up."

"It might be wise to try and salvage whatever alien artifacts you can. A holographic projector, and as many cubes as you can find, could be invaluable in disproving the wild accusation that the Selestians are a hoax," suggested Duncan, as he put on his helmet.

"Got your pistol?" asked Hawkins.

"You bet!" replied Thompson.

"Good hunting," said Erica, as the two men entered the air lock. "We'll meet you down the road."

"Hopefully, in this life," Marina whispered to Hawkins, as she finished suturing and bandaging his wound.

Exiting the green door, the pursuers viewed the empty outer chamber. The Rover, of course, was nowhere to be found. As they passed through the open door of the "Face," they gazed out into a bleak Martian landscape bathed in the pinkish glow of early dawn. It would take the exertion of a fast running pace to ward off the bitter chill in the thin atmosphere. Orienting himself, Thompson pointed out the direction they must take in order to reach the Questor by the shortest possible route. Never, in all history, had there been a ten-kilometer obstacle foot race with so much at stake.

With their helmet radios set to a different frequency, they would not risk the chance of Alvarez picking up any random chatter once they came within range. The element of surprise was a key weapon at their disposal, as there was no reason for their quarry to suspect that he might be intercepted.

"How much time do we have before the next launch window opens up?" asked Duncan, over his radio link.

"A little under an hour and a half."

"It's going to be awfully close."

"I know."

"Incidentally, I think I've figured out how Alvarez was able to con us into a wild goose chase - causing us to look for Manzoni in the wrong direction - while also serving the purpose of seeming to eliminate himself as a suspect," said Duncan, increasing the pace as they reached a relatively level stretch of ground.

"How?"

"After Marina arrived to tend to Hawkins, I happened to notice that Manzoni's communicator was set on channel 44. I do believe it was Talon's radio, or else they observed the different setting and decided to monitor our security channel. In either case, they likely overheard our conversations and acted accordingly."

"That would certainly explain how they always managed to be one step ahead of us."

"It also allowed Alvarez to get the jump on both Niemeyer and Talon, as he was not considered a suspect."

"Who would ever have expected Alvarez to be in league with the fanatics?" lamented Thompson. "His record as an astronaut was most impeccable."

"I imagine that some heads will roll back home for failure to uncover his involvement with such a nefarious group - assuming, of course, that we manage to get news of his treachery to our buddies aboard the Celeste."

"This race could well end in a photo finish," said Thompson, panting slightly as the two pursuers climbed out of yet another eroded impact crater.

"We appear to be making good time, all things considered. How much of a head start do you think he got on us?" Duncan asked.

"Probably not more than a few minutes, as he would have lost some time in stopping to open the outer door of the alien complex. He will lose even more by having to cycle both into and out of the Rover's air lock."

"On the other side of the coin, I would estimate that the Rover is able to travel about twice as fast as our present speed. How much do you think this short cut will save us?"

"Almost half, I should say."

"I see what you mean by a photo finish."

"If Alvarez should ever manage to get away with it, what kind of a lame excuse do you suppose he is prepared to give Tanaka and

Karanov?" asked Thompson.

"Most likely he'll try to claim that he was sent back to the Questor, in order to pick up supplies, when our fool physicists began tampering with the alien matter/antimatter reactor - causing a massive radiation leak and an impending explosion."

"And being warned of this, by his colleagues who had already incurred a fatal radiation dose, he alone was ordered to escape before it was too late," added Thompson, completing the story.

"Exactly!"

"Do you think they'll buy it?"

"They might. In fact, it would fit right in with a suspicion that Manzoni intended to sabotage the alien complex."

"We've got to catch him," said Thompson, more determined than ever to do so by stepping up the pace another notch.

With great loping strides, which saw them literally bounding over the rugged terrain, they had now covered considerably more than half of the intervening distance to the Questor. Without a compass as a guide they had to hope that their sense of direction would not fail them. There was little room for error, and the constant need to detour around large boulders and steep walled mini-craters did not help matters. Whenever they began to exhibit signs of exhaustion, the very thought of all that was at stake served to spur them onward.

When they were within an estimated one kilometer of reaching their objective misfortune struck. In attempting to leap over a small crater Thompson's left foot came down hard on a cluster of rocks, twisting his ankle and sending him sprawling.

"Are you all right, Adam?" Duncan asked, stopping to assist his friend.

"It's my ankle," Thompson said, wincing in pain after he put weight on it and tried to run.

Supporting his comrade, Duncan endeavored to help.

"It's no use, Matt, you'll have to go on without me. Here, take the gun; it will now be up to you to stop him. I'll hobble along as best I can."

Taking the pistol, Duncan sprinted on ahead, hoping that this momentary delay would not prove fatal. Upon reaching the top of a nearby hill, he looked down to see the Questor, somewhat less than a kilometer to his right and a few hundred meters in front of him. He could also view the Rover, as it was pulling to a stop close to their spacecraft.

"I see him, Adam. He's just arrived, but has yet to cycle through the air lock."

"You'll have to shoot the moment you think you can hit him. You have eleven shots left out of a clip of twelve. If you could approach from behind you may be able to catch him unawares."

Heeding the advice, Duncan made straight for the rear of the Rover, lest his prey glimpse him with a turn of the head. He had closed to a distance of little more than a hundred meters when Alvarez exited the vehicle's air lock. He was some twenty meters or so from the Questor's entrance ramp, and walking briskly with his back toward him.

Cresting a hill, Thompson could see the drama about to unfold. "Fire a few shots at him, Matt. Even if you miss, he'll never hear them in this exceedingly thin atmosphere and enclosed in his suit," he urged.

While sprinting at top speed, with his legs beginning to feel quite rubbery, Duncan managed to squeeze off three shots in rapid succession. Alvarez continued to move ahead. Closing to within fifty meters, he fired three more times. His quarry still did not respond in any way. Presently only a few meters short of reaching the ramp, it was clearly a case of now or never. Coming to a halt at a distance of about forty meters, he took careful aim and fired another burst of three shots. Alvarez seemed to stumble and turn in his direction before pitching over and falling to the ground.

"You got him!" Thompson shouted, over their radio link.

"Hallelujah!" exclaimed Duncan, resuming his race toward the Questor's open ramp.

Finding Alvarez as good as dead, with multiple chest wounds, Duncan quickly retraced his steps to assist Thompson, who was limping rather badly. By the time they reached the ramp, leading to the interior of the Questor, it was evident that they would be extremely hard pressed to make the narrow launch window, now less than forty minutes away. The next opportunity to rendezvous with the Celeste would not be until long after the "Face" was scheduled to explode.

"Take the Rover and pick up the others while I make certain launch preparations," said Thompson. "I can climb up the ladder by myself."

Cycling through the Rover's air lock, it was not long before Duncan had the vehicle turned and was racing against time. At top speed it was capable of barely more than 30 kilometers per hour. Performing some quick mental arithmetic, he didn't see how he could win. Adam, his close friend and colleague, must have known that returning for the others would almost certainly preclude a successful rendezvous launch before the "Face" exploded. The big question in his mind was the magnitude of this impending disaster. Could the Questor survive the blast without damage? Would the release of massive amounts of radiation do them in? He simply did not know.

After traveling some 14 kilometers, according to the Rover's odometer, he spotted three figures trotting toward him. Stopping momentarily to pick them up, and without waiting for his comrades to cycle through the air lock, Duncan reversed direction and sped back toward the Questor at maximum speed. They had won the first and most crucial race to stop Alvarez; but this second race was destined to be one which they would surely lose.

"How big an explosion do you think it will be, Brian?" asked Duncan, after Hawkins had emerged from the air lock and removed his protective helmet.

"Does this mean that we may miss the launch window?" inquired the physicist.

"I'm afraid so."

"Then you should have saved yourselves by lifting off without us," voiced Erica, her long blonde hair hanging down to the helmet which she now held in her lap. It was a sentiment expressed by both Marina and Hawkins.

"No way! We're all in this mess together. Besides, if I know Adam, he'll find some way to get us out of this admittedly sticky situation," said Duncan, wondering himself how he might do so.

The optimum window for an intercept launch had come and gone by the time Duncan brought the Rover to a stop near the entrance ramp to the Questor. "Let's gather up our luggage and get out of here," he said.

"We managed to bring two of the Selestian holograph projectors and a dozen cubes," remarked Erica.

"And I have samples as well as the formula for the promised longevity elixir," added Marina. "But it's too bad we couldn't salvage one of the alien's cancer killing machines."

"Regrettably, our scientists will have to solve the hydrogen fusion problem all by themselves," lamented Hawkins.

"We did all that we could, and half a loaf is still better than none," said Duncan, reaching for his helmet.

At this moment Thompson's voice came over the Rover's radio speaker: "No need to risk breaking your necks scrambling up the ladder, since our flight will be delayed somewhat. Incidentally, it would be appreciated if the last one up would turn off and unplug the power supply from our nuclear reactor. I've got the cabin heated to a comfortable level."

"Will do," said Duncan. "See you shortly."

"We missed our final intercept opportunity by a little over ten minutes," Thompson announced, as the last of his four fellow crew members entered the control cabin of the Questor's upper stage and had removed their helmets.

"What options do we have?" inquired Duncan.

"We have exactly two: One, we stay put until the next launch window, and risk being destroyed in the blast or by the radiation. Two, we launch before the explosion and take our chances on making a later rendezvous with the Celeste," said Thompson.

"Which do you recommend?" asked Marina.

"Can you give me a reliable estimate, Brian, of the thermal energy and radiation output of the explosion?" Thompson wanted to know. "I can allow you ten minutes to come up with an answer."

Pulling a notebook out of his jacket pocket, with his good arm, Hawkins began to study it intently. Punching figures into the ship's computer, it was not long before a series of numbers were displayed on a video screen - none of which seemed to be very pleasing to the physicist.

"What's the verdict?" asked Thompson.

"I think the sooner we get out of here the better," answered Hawkins. "The amount of energy likely to be released is far in excess of an extremely powerful hydrogen bomb. There's just no way that we could survive such a blast at our distance. Moreover, the situation gets even worse when radiation is considered, as the flux of liberated gamma rays alone is positively staggering. In order to be adequately shielded we will have to be well below the horizon when it blows."

"Will Phobos do? I've already programmed a launch to this inner satellite in exactly four minutes," Thompson informed them.

"Phobos would do nicely as a shield," said Hawkins.

"I've always wanted to visit this particular moon," confided Marina.

"Fortunately, the Celeste will be on the other side of the planet when the explosion occurs, so our comrades will be quite safe. The big unanswered question is going to be what happens once we get there," Thompson added.

"You mean that we might not be able to reach the Celeste?" asked Erica.

"Or vice versa," said Thompson. "In any event, I must inform you all that I managed to contact Tanaka and give him a rather brief synopsis of events. I should imagine that by now the news is producing more than a little excitement back on Earth."

"If Manzoni was telling us the truth we have only about forty minutes before the explosion," remarked Duncan.

"Better strap yourselves in," advised Thompson. "We launch in precisely one minute."

Sixty seconds passed quickly, terminating with a sudden jolt that pushed the astronauts deep into their contoured seats, five of which remained vacant for the return trip. Within a minute the Martian surface lay tens of kilometers below them. In a few more minutes diminutive Phobos appeared on one of their video screens, growing noticeably larger as they watched. The relatively huge crater, Stickney, was clearly perceptible. Some 10 kilometers in diameter, it totally dominated the landscape of a moon averaging only 22 kilometers across.

"Have a good look at the crater while you can, because that's the last we're going to see of it for now," said Thompson. "Since Stickney always presents its face to Mars, we cannot stay on this side as it will be exposed to the predicted discharge of gamma ray radiation."

Closing fast on the Martian satellite, Thompson oriented the

Questor's ascent stage with a few short bursts from the craft's maneuvering nozzles. A longer burn with their single liquid fuel rocket engine inserted them into orbit around the tiny moon. As they passed behind Phobos, yet another burn killed their orbital motion and allowed the weak gravity of the body to slowly draw them toward its surface.

"It can explode any time now and we'll be safe," Thompson was finally able to announce.

"How will we know if it does explode?" Marina asked.

"We won't be able to tell from here, but the Celeste will be in a position to do so," answered Thompson. We should establish contact with them in about forty minutes. By then it will likely be all over and we'll be able to enter into a normal orbit around Phobos."

"Too bad we can't land on the satellite," remarked Hawkins.

"Regrettably, our engineers never considered the need to visit Phobos. Our upper stage simply doesn't have any legs to stand on, so we'll have to hover until the danger is past," said Thompson.

"Fortunately, in the weak gravity of the satellite, it will not require an inordinate amount of fuel in the short time that we must hide on the back side of the moon," elaborated Erica.

The waiting game was now on. Eventually, after their craft had dropped some distance toward the surface, a short burst of a few seconds at low throttle soon restored them to their desired altitude. Until such time as rotation of the Red Planet would carry the "Face" away from their line of sight, or the Celeste could confirm its detonation, they would be compelled to play a game of slowly bobbing up and down above the surface of Phobos.

"Why didn't we simply go into orbit about Mars?" asked Marina. "We could have been well over the horizon at the time of the big explosion."

"We could have indeed avoided the impending blast by doing just that. However, it would also put us into an orbit from which we would have no hope of a rendezvous with the Celeste," Thompson explained.

"I see," said Marina.

"Unfortunately, we're not out of the woods yet," Thompson was obliged to reveal. "While there is a definite chance of linking up with the Celeste, in our present orbit, it is far from an ideal situation. In particular, the retrograde motion of Phobos tends to complicate matters somewhat. I would much prefer to have been shielded behind Deimos - except that it was impossible for us to reach in view of our need to make a hasty departure."

Time seemed to drag on and on during the course of the bobbing game. At last a message came through from the Celeste. They had trained their instruments on the "Face" - or at least the region where it was. All their radar could detect, through a great plume of dust, was an uncharted crater - one estimated to be at least 30 kilometers in diameter!

"I wonder what members of the Galactic Society will have to say about this shocking act of violence," said Erica, thoroughly disgusted by man's gross stupidity and ignorance.

"When they do find out they will surely place us near the very bottom of their list of potential candidates, and I wouldn't blame them at all," opined Duncan.

"It makes me ashamed to be associated with the human race," commented Hawkins. "I had so hoped that my calculations would prove to be in error."

"This loss to society is truly without precedent, and a crime of the highest magnitude," pronounced Marina.

"I subscribe to all of the above," said Thompson, turning his attention to a cluster of instruments.

With the hovering act over, it was time to stop wasting their precious fuel in periodic attempts to offset the gravitational pull of Phobos. It had now become expedient to enter into some kind of orbit around the satellite - preferably one that would best facilitate a rendezvous with the Celeste. Their onboard computer soon prescribed a trajectory which offered a number of later options. A more detailed intercept program would have to await a solution through Mission Control's more sophisticated arsenal of computers.

"All right, folks, one stable Phobos orbit coming up," said Thompson, activating maneuvering jets which turned the Questor and oriented it in the proper position. "We're about to get a scenic view of Stickney."

A short burst with the craft's main thruster soon inserted them into an almost circular orbit around the Martian moon. How long they would stay in such an orbit remained to be seen. If lack of fuel should preclude a rescue by the Celeste, they would become a perpetual monument to mankind's treachery and lack of maturity.

Informing Tanaka of their orbital coordinates and fuel reserve - along with statistics involving such consumables as air, water and food - Thompson could only sit back and await the verdict from Mission Control. Into the equation of life or death would go the fuel status of the Celeste and the need to depart for home by a certain date. Meanwhile, they were advised to catch up on missed sleep and let Earth's orbital specialists work out an intercept plan. As a worse case scenario, they could at least reflect that they had managed to save a handful of valuable Selestian artifacts - even if it should take a third expedition to the Red Planet in order to retrieve them.

"I wonder if it would be wise to withhold news of the salvaged alien treasures from the general public - at least until certain aspects of this bizarre situation can be studied in depth," voiced Duncan.

"Why?" asked Marina.

"Offhand, I can think of several reasons. First, the fanatics have staked their reputation upon the wild accusation that alien contact is all a big hoax. If we let them go on making a host of absurd claims, and then abruptly pull the rug out from under them, they will suffer a dramatic and devastating loss of face," replied Duncan. "Second, it will enhance public outcry when they think of all that has been thrown away. The stronger this resentment the more likely governments will be to clamp down on the fanatics. Finally, the very knowledge that we are returning, with a number of priceless artifacts, can only serve to inspire desperate acts of additional sabotage."

"That's all we would need!" exclaimed Hawkins.

"Heaven only knows how many different groups of terrorists there are running around loose," said Erica.

"Indeed," agreed Thompson. "The failure of our drag-chute to deploy seemed to come as a complete surprise to Alvarez. If it was sabotaged, as I strongly suspect, then it was the work of a separate party."

"Evidently, at least two different factions are involved," deduced Marina.

"Make that probably no less than three," said Thompson. "I later found out that the one fellow they caught, in the act of trying to sabotage a valve on the Questor, could not possibly have had access to the drag-chute compartment."

"No wonder the terrorists seemed confident that our mission would fail. They had saboteurs everywhere - from technicians to crew!" declared Hawkins, thoroughly exasperated.

"I think your idea to restrict knowledge of the salvaged alien artifacts makes a great deal of sense, Matt," Thompson responded. "What I propose to do is to inform Tanaka and Karamov of what we managed to save, and have them relay this information in a special code that only Stanwick and a few trusted subordinates at Mission Control can decipher."

"Does Tanaka have the code?" Duncan asked.

"I gave him the necessary instructions just before we left the Celeste," replied Thompson.

"Let's hope that we can give the terrorists enough rope to hang themselves," remarked Erica.

"Speaking of rope, we have both the means and opportunity to check out the reason for the drag-chute failure," said Thompson. "The compartment was inaccessible while we were on the surface; but in space it will be a simple matter to float over to it and have a close look."

"Couldn't you drift away and get lost?" asked Marina.

"Not when I'm secured by a rope," replied Thompson, opening a storage compartment and producing a considerable length of strong nylon cord.

"I didn't know we carried such an item," said Hawkins.

"Four years ago Chadwick taught me the wisdom of including rope when exploring a strange planet," chuckled Thompson.

Anxious to confirm his suspicion, it was not long before the intrepid astronaut exited the air lock of the Questor. With one end of the rope clipped securely to his utility belt, Thompson proceeded to fasten the other end to a rung on the ladder which extended the length of the craft's central passageway. Reaching the exterior of the hull, he was grateful for handholds that allowed him to climb to the far side of the ship. As he passed the windows of the control cabin he waved to his colleagues, who could not resist video taping the scene.

"I suppose you plan on submitting this caper to one of the major news channels," remarked Thompson, over his helmet radio.

"Could you oblige by doing a rope commercial?" Erica retorted.

Clutching the drag-chute hatch, Thompson struggled to unbolt the cover. Eventually succeeding, he peered inside. It did not require an experienced engineer to discover the trouble. Grasping one end of a severed wire in his gloved fingers, he could tell at a glance that it had been deliberately cut through. Once again, he could not help wondering if other surprises might lie in store.

Chapter 10

TRIBULATION AND RETRIBUTION

Within 24 hours of the Questor going into orbit around Phobos, a reply was received from Mission Control, routed to them via the Celeste. The transmission included both good news and bad news. The good news was that a rendezvous with the mother ship would be possible some four days hence. The bad news was that it was bound to leave them without sufficient fuel for the customary mid-course correction, and for later insertion into proper Earth orbit. This virtually sealed the fate of the Celeste, although it was deemed feasible to rescue the crew by means of an intercept shuttle that could be launched from either Prometheus or Lunar Colony. Since they would have nearly six months in which to make a decision, this detail could best be resolved at a later date.

The four days eventually passed, seeming more like four weeks in the restricted confinement of the Questor's tiny control cabin. Even with only five out of the original ten astronauts returning, it did not alter the fact that the craft was designed as a short term shuttle from orbit to the surface and back.

"I'm picking up the Celeste on the radar screen," announced Erica.

"Time to get out of here at long last," said Thompson, as he initiated a burn with the ship's single liquid fuel engine.

Some forty minutes earlier, Karamov had ignited a total of four solid fuel rockets, in order to change both direction and velocity. A substantial burn with the Celeste's twin liquid fuel engines succeeded in very nearly matching the retrograde motion of Phobos. If all went well a limited burn with the Questor's small fuel reserve would allow the two craft to effect a rendezvous in less than an hour.

This time interval appeared to pass at a much faster rate, as they awaited the moment when an intercept would either occur or end in failure. If the experts at Mission Control had made even a small error it could spell the end for those aboard the Questor. There would be no second chance due to an extreme shortage of any maneuvering fuel. All five crew members inwardly dreaded the very real possibility of something going awry.

"We have the Celeste on our external video camera," declared Duncan.

"Closing speed 44 meters per second," advised Erica.

"How much fuel do you have left?" asked Tanaka, over their radio link.

"Next to zero, I'm afraid," replied Thompson. "How are you guys fixed for the same commodity?"

"You don't want to know," came the voice of Karamov.

"That bad?" Thompson responded.

"We should be able to kill our approach velocity, but I would prefer that any maneuvering be done by the Questor," announced the Russian pilot.

"Just make sure that you conserve enough fuel for your wing jet thrusters," reminded Thompson. "The Celeste will need to make at least two major orientation maneuvers if we are to enter into any kind of Earth orbit."

"Understood," replied Karamov.

Some ten minutes later the two craft lay drifting together in Mars orbit, less than forty meters apart. As Thompson endeavored to dock with the Celeste he was dismayed to find that there was no response from the Questor's thrusters.

"So close and yet so far," commented Duncan. "Are we going to have to get out and push?"

"I suppose we'll have to do something. If we wait for gravity to draw us closer we could be here for quite some time," remarked Thompson.

"What are our options?" asked Hawkins.

"I think I can guess," said Erica, as she observed Thompson making his way toward a certain storage locker.

"Might it be the old rope trick?" inquired Duncan.

"It could indeed be a case of rope to the rescue," responded Thompson, again producing his coil of sturdy nylon cord.

"Do you really plan to launch yourself over to the Celeste's air lock?" asked Marina.

"That's the general idea," Thompson replied. "I only hope this rope is long enough."

Minutes later Thompson exited the Questor with his trusty rope fastened to a utility belt, having first secured the other end to the bottom rung of the passageway ladder. Also attached to his belt was an oxygen tank, its mass essentially negated by the state of weightlessness induced by free fall in space. Deftly launching himself toward the Celeste, he used occasional bursts of escaping oxygen gas to direct his flight. He need only grasp a firm hold upon any portion of the mother ship in order to literally pull the two craft together.

"Your trajectory is looking good," reported Erica, monitoring the escapade.

Heading straight for the Celeste's air lock, Thompson received a minor setback when the line went taut some three meters short of his destination. "Plan B coming up," he announced over his helmet radio.

"Exactly, what is such a plan?" asked Tanaka, likewise noting the drama now transpiring.

"It has something to do with the old saying of any port in a storm," said Thompson, opening up the valve on his oxygen tank. Pointing it so as to induce thrust toward a nearby wing pod of solid fuel rockets, it was not long before he managed to clutch one of the connecting struts.

"Your Buck Rogers flying belt trick seems to have worked very well," remarked Duncan. "Next, I suppose you'll want to impress us with your rendition of Hercules pulling a spaceship."

"Not until you promise to video tape the caper," Thompson jested, as he consolidated his grip in preparation for the big pull.

"Lights, camera, action! Our ham actor is about to perform," declared Erica, as Marina proceeded to tape the spectacle.

Thompson began to tug on the rope. In response, the distance between the two craft slowly diminished. Obtaining sufficient slack, he once more launched himself toward the Celeste's air lock. Reaching his objective, he promptly fastened the rope to a convenient handhold located inside the chamber.

"He did it!" exclaimed Hawkins.

"Grab helmets and luggage, folks, and prepare to board your new home for the next six months," said Thompson. "Just remember to have one hand firmly on the rope at all times."

Gathering up their treasures, it was not long before the four remaining astronauts were making their way in single file across the dark abyss of space. The Questor had served them well, and it was not without some sadness that they now left the small craft as a monument of their narrow escape to Phobos.

Receiving a hearty welcome from Tanaka and Karamov, Thompson and his group of survivors wasted little time in relaying a news update to Mission Control. Conveniently passing over the region of the "Face," during their TV broadcast, they could not resist the temptation to beam back pictures of the blast site. Clearly visible, through their telephoto lense, was a hitherto unknown and as yet unnamed crater which measured a full 30 kilometers across! This great depression would forever stand as mute testimony to the gross stupidity and ignorance of mankind. In the name of religion the human race had destroyed a truly priceless gift - one which could have advanced the cause of Earth society by many centuries.

With nothing further to be gained from remaining any longer in Mars orbit, and having already obtained numerous close-up pictures of Phobos, it was decided to depart for home at first opportunity. Taking advantage of a convenient launch window, which opened some four hours after concluding the TV session, Thompson ignited a series of solid fuel rockets, sending the Celeste on a long spiral trajectory toward Earth. Unable to effect the usual mid-course correction, due to lack of liquid propellant, only time would tell what sort of Earth orbit (if any) might be forthcoming.

One week after commencing the lengthy voyage home, Hawkins was motivated to have a serious discussion with Thompson. Reasoning that Manzoni had over a month of freedom in which to perpetrate an act of sabotage, before Stanwick's warning had been received, he felt justified in mentioning a rather disconcerting possibility which had come to mind.

"You really believe he could have installed such a device?" asked Thompson, somewhat shaken by his colleague's theory.

"If he was able to do it once he could surely have done it twice," replied Hawkins. "It would serve as a back-up plan to guarantee that the Celeste would never return to Earth."

"I see what you mean. If their escape went as intended, it would be a simple matter for him to remove the device during the return trip. On the other hand, if he did not make it back to the Celeste, then the mother ship would never be allowed to reach Earth," Thompson deduced.

"Exactly!"

"I think we'd better check this out immediately. Assuming a worst case scenario, how much time will you likely need to effect repairs?"

Hawkins thought for a moment before replying. "Probably not much more than thirty minutes or so," he said.

Activating the ship's intercom system, Thompson proceeded to make the following announcement: "In about ten minutes we will go on emergency battery power for a brief interval while we shut down our reactor. We need to make certain that Manzoni didn't try the same stunt aboard the Celeste."

Gathering up an assortment of tools, Hawkins and Thompson were soon on their way down the long passageway leading to the nuclear reactor, which was situated at the extreme rear of the spacecraft. Geiger counter and flashlights in hand, they opened the door to the compartment housing the ship's main power source. Removing the reactor's cover, the two men peered anxiously inside.

"Damn!" Thompson cursed, as he gazed upon what was clearly a timing mechanism of some sort.

"Looks like a repeat performance," voiced Hawkins.

"When is it set to trigger a meltdown?" Thompson was quick to ask.

"About seven weeks from now," replied Hawkins, following his careful examination of the timing device.

"Just a month after we would have been on our way back home."

"And with plenty of time for Manzoni to have safely removed the trigger had all gone according to plan," Hawkins added.

"Any problem in disconnecting it?" asked Thompson.

"Piece of cake. However, I will say one thing about this most insidious device," remarked Hawkins, cutting the two wires which linked it to a nearby servo motor.

"What's that?"

"There's no way that he could have fabricated it from any of the supplies or spare components belonging to the Celeste."

"You mean it must have been smuggled aboard already assembled and as a separate item?"

"Indeed I do," Hawkins answered. "Furthermore, he would have needed another conspirator to have done so, since all our personal hand luggage was supposedly checked before leaving Prometheus."

"This entire expedition seems characterized by a redundancy of plans to do us in."

"You're telling me! Say, shine that light over here, Adam, I need to connect these two wires to the safeguard mechanism which our friend chose to bypass."

"I wonder how Mission Control will react to this most recent flaunting of their security measures," remarked Thompson.

"There seems to be an inordinate number of fanatics branching out into space," commented Hawkins.

"And I used to think that Earth was the sole domain of crazy zealots and terrorists," admitted Thompson, more than a little disenchanted with human nature in general.

"We've certainly had our share of trials and tribulations," agreed the physicist.

"You know, Brian, I think Matt was right when he once rather jokingly referred to Earth as a purgatory planet."

"I won't give you any argument on that assessment."

Leaving the reactor room some minutes later, it was not long before power was restored and functions aboard the Celeste had returned to normal. Relaying news of the thwarted sabotage plot to Mission Control, they sat back and awaited the response. But as days became weeks, nothing was heard which would indicate that any accomplices had been apprehended.

When they did receive a report concerning Manzoni's friends and associates, at about the same time that the Celeste's reactor was programmed for meltdown, it was to learn that his wife had just been diagnosed with terminal cancer. How utterly ironic, they thought, that a gift from the Selestians - which could have saved her life - had been vaporized by her husband in the name of religion!

Compelled by a shortage of liquid propellant to forgo any mid-course correction, the Celeste hurtled onward in a long spiral arc to intercept the orbit of their home planet. As month followed month they drew ever closer to the moment when ignition of their solid fuel rockets would allow them to be captured by Earth's gravity. That point in time had now arrived.

"This is it, fellow astronauts," declared Thompson, as he oriented the big ship in preparation for a final series of rocket burns.

According to latest calculations, the ideal amount of thrust required to effect a rendezvous did not correspond to a multiple of any number of their rockets. Instead, it involved utilizing all but 20% of the thrust generated by a single rocket. Too much thrust could be almost as bad as too little. By way of solution, it was decided to make use of the explosive bolts in the lattice framework which secured the rockets to the wing pods. If their timing was right it should be possible to rid the Celeste of this unneeded thrust by cutting the last pair loose while 10% of each rocket's propellant still remained. Such a plan would consume the last vestiges of their fuel.

"How eccentric do you think our orbit will be?" asked Duncan, as the jettisoned pair of rockets shot away from the ship, and the astronauts once more returned to a state of free fall.

"It'll be a few hours before Mission Control can give us an accurate assessment of our trajectory," Thompson announced. "But I shouldn't be surprised if we swing out well beyond the Moon's orbit at apogee."

"What about perigee? How close will we come to Earth?" Marina inquired.

"Probably between 50,000 and 100,000 kilometers. Again, it won't be known for certain until we've been tracked for several hours," replied Thompson.

One day after entering into a rather eccentric Earth orbit, ranging from 80,000 to almost 700,000 kilometers, a rescue plan was submitted by Mission Control. It called for the dispatch of a lunar shuttle from Prometheus some two days hence. Instead of returning to Earth's orbiting space station, however, they would stop over at Lunar Colony for refueling. If all went according to schedule, the Mars adventurers were expected to arrive home by the end of the following week.

Four days after capture by Earth's gravitational field, the seven remaining crew members of the Celeste were rescued by the Copernicus. Pride of the small lunar shuttle fleet, it had been fitted with extra fuel tanks for the mission. Pulling alongside, it was only a matter of minutes before the two craft had docked and a seal made between their respective air locks. The transfer of crew and treasure was accomplished without incident and the two ships soon parted company. Hopefully, at some future date, the Celeste could be recovered and refurbished for yet another Martian expedition, as it was a good ship that had performed well in both of its voyages to the Red Planet.

"I sure hate to abandon the Celeste," lamented Thompson, as the Copernicus initiated a rocket burn with its twin liquid fuel engines.

"I've always wanted to visit the Moon," said Marina, watching their home for the past six months dwindle to a small speck of light amidst a starry background.

Forty hours later the Copernicus hovered over Lunar Colony, slowly descending toward a marker placed at the center of a surrounding cluster of dwellings sunk into the soil of the crater Alphonsus. A radio telescope and a dome housing a respectable optical counterpart were clearly visible through the shuttle's windows. Just when the rescued passengers were beginning to enjoy the scenery, their view was obscured by large amounts of dust kicked up by the craft's engine exhaust.

Shortly after the last of the debris had settled, two space-suited figures appeared dragging an accordion-style tube which measured some two meters in diameter. The open end was promptly attached to the air lock of the Copernicus; while the other was seen to disappear into the ground, approximately ten meters away.

"We are now free to enter the umbilical tube leading to our underground air lock," announced Frank Morgan, pilot of the rescue shuttle, upon observing a flashing green light on a nearby control panel.

"How sophisticated!" exclaimed Marina. "We don't even have to don our space suits."

"Nothing but the best for our hero guests," remarked Samantha Jackson, copilot of the Copernicus.

Entering the underground complex of tunnels and chambers, the seven returning Mars astronauts were accorded a hero's welcome. All 28 members of the international consortium of lunar scientists and technicians were on hand to greet them. Escorted on a tour of the recently constructed establishment, they were impressed by the engineering feats which had transformed a bleak and airless world into a habitable base for research and astronomical exploration. When compared to that of the Selestian's Martian "Face," however, the contrast was quite overwhelming. The very thought of what had been lost - through sheer ignorance and stupidity - was enough to haunt the crew of the Celeste for the rest of their lives!

The salvaged alien treasures, carefully concealed inside their personal luggage, continued to remain a secret to all but Stanwick and a handful of his trusted associates. In a highly publicized television interview with the Mars astronauts, later that same day, there was still no mention made of any Selestian artifacts. This decision to withhold information seemed amply justified by the claims of many religious leaders, who persisted in maintaining that contact with an alien civilization was all a great hoax to discredit orthodox theology. It was deemed prudent to wait until the crew of the Celeste had returned safely to Earth before news of the artifacts was disclosed.

The following day, refreshed and rested, all seven of the rescued adventurers were invited to dine with the director of Lunar Colony. Donald T. Hartman, a noted radio astronomer in his mid forties, was a rather jovial scientist of medium height and build. To Duncan's delight, he possessed a keen interest in both philosophy and cosmology. His wife, Irene, an attractive brunette in her late thirties, was a computer specialist with a background in astronomy. The two appeared to make an excellent team, and had evidently come to be highly regarded by their colleagues.

"Did Donald mention that we recently discovered a promising deposit of water, in the form of permafrost, at a depth of some forty meters?" Hartman's wife asked, as she set a large bowl of steamed brown rice on the table beside dishes containing carrots, broccoli and turkey - all of which had been reconstituted from a dehydrated state.

"Please help yourselves," interjected her husband. "While it's still astronaut food, I must say that Irene does have a way with our microwave oven."

"I did hear something about plans to start open pit mining a few months from now," responded Tanaka. "How will you power your bulldozers?"

"Strictly electrical power," Hartman answered. "The batteries will be recharged from our nuclear reactor buried about a hundred meters away from our habitation modules."

"Have precautions been taken to guard against the possibility of sabotage?" Hawkins was quick to inquire.

"As a matter of fact, the unfortunate experience with your portable reactor did cause us to adopt protective measures. In addition to a locked door and a secret alarm system, the room is off limits to all but a handful of personnel. Even then, it is necessary for three of us to be present in order to gain access," Hartman elaborated.

"How well have the residents of Lunar Colony been screened for their religious affiliations?" asked Thompson.

"We don't think any of the fanatics have managed to infiltrate the base," Hartman responded. "However, I must admit that it was a considerable shock to learn about Alvarez's treachery. He was one of the last persons I might have suspected."

"What do you suppose makes a man lose all sense of reason and go completely berserk?" Irene Hartman wanted to know.

"In the case of Alvarez and Manzoni, I rather expect it was because they were unable to face the fact that their cherished religious beliefs were in error, opined Professor Duncan. "In the last analysis all sin, no matter how disguised, may be traced to an immature state of mind - one in which selfishness is allowed to prevail over a desire for truth. To admit error is to degrade an individual's worth in terms of self-esteem. Thus an immature soul will resist correction, very often supporting ideas and beliefs totally lacking in logic and common sense, in order to bolster or protect one's ego."

"What makes it so pathetic is that many of the fanatics are such outwardly staunch supporters of popular religious dogma - whereas inwardly their fear of conceding falsehood tends to make them unstable and dangerous to others who would dare to point out their error," remarked Erica.

"Nor is this fear of loss of prestige confined to religious individuals," continued the professor. "It very much extends to all branches of science. By way of illustration, we still have a preponderance of believers in the Big Bang theory of creation - long past the point where an impartial look at the evidence would reveal it to be without foundation and contrary to observation."

"Objection of the very rich to the Selestian's philosophy and economic precepts is clearly based upon plain selfishness, as they are simply unwilling to share their undeserved wealth with others. To them, material rewards are more important than spiritual values or inner worth," Erica stated, helping herself to an ample serving of broccoli, her favorite vegetable.

"For where your treasure is, there will your heart be also," quoted Duncan, from words attributed to Jesus. "It has always amazed me how many wealthy persons profess to be Christians, and yet refuse to accept the principle conveyed by this excellent proverb."

"I believe such people are known as hypocrites," Erica could not resist adding.

It was at this point that Hartman raised an issue that the Mars adventurers would have preferred to evade. "It's a pity that you couldn't have brought back one of those incredible miniature holographic projectors that you reported in your broadcast, just prior to the explosion threat," he said.

Avoiding the temptation to reveal their treasures prematurely, even to those whom they trusted, Thompson replied: "We had so very little time, in which to race Alvarez to the Questor, that any salvaging of Selestian artifacts was quite secondary. But I will say that we hope to disprove claims that alien contact is a hoax."

Satisfied with the explanation, talk was soon channeled to a description of the inner chambers of the "Face," and of prospects that Earth might receive a visit from one of the great starships some centuries into the future.

Three days after arriving at Lunar Colony, the seven survivors departed on the shuttle Copernicus, en route to Earth via Space Station Prometheus. The trip was quite uneventful, and two days later they received a hero's welcome aboard the same satellite base from whence they had commenced their journey some ten months earlier.

Although the mission could only be described as a disaster, it was not a complete failure. While the few paltry artifacts that they had managed to salvage were small compensation for what might have been, it was hoped that an aroused populace would soon be stimulated to embrace the Selestian's superior wisdom with respect to philosophy/religion. There was also the prospect that Earth society would be motivated to adopt many of the political/economic reforms advocated by the alien civilization. Only time would tell if this would indeed be the case.

Such thoughts were very much on the minds of the Celeste's crew as they were interviewed by awaiting news media. Repeating their accounts of treachery and destruction of the "Face," they continued to withhold information regarding the alien treasures now concealed in their luggage. Instead, they elaborated at great length upon the loss of the promised cure for cancer, along with failure to bring back the secret for controlled hydrogen fusion. The ironic twist of fate concerning Manzoni's wife, currently given only another month to live, was a topic readily seized upon by the TV reporters. It was not difficult to imagine the strong emotional reaction of the countless millions of individuals whose households had been plagued with the grim specter of this dreaded malady.

Sensing a growing public outcry against those who would deny the truth of alien contact, evangelist Graham James was prompt to respond with a multinetwork TV broadcast aimed at offsetting this resentment. Not only did he continue to reiterate the wild "hoax" hypothesis, but he was driven to claim that the Selestian "Face" was deliberately destroyed in order to: "cover up the blasphemer's inability to bring back treasurers which simply did not exist!" Their so-called portable nuclear reactor was, he claimed, really a powerful hydrogen bomb. Furthermore, he maintained, the five dead crew members were probably murdered when they opposed their plan to detonate the nuclear device. Before the day had ended there were large numbers of confused viewers and a raging controversy between rival camps.

The following morning the Mars astronauts boarded a routine shuttle flight bound for Cape Canaveral, arriving at exactly 10 A.M. local time. The welcoming committee, while an enthusiastic group, was necessarily limited in number and subject to a very strict security check. It would not do to have come so far - and endured so much - to be done in by a crazed terrorist at the last moment. On hand to greet them were presidents or vice presidents of all participating nations, along with Andrew L. Stanwick of Mission Control.

Also anxiously awaiting the adventurers were immediate family members of the astronauts, including Janet Thompson and her two children, Susan and Robert. With no quarantine needed, they were allowed a hasty embrace before being hustled off for a debriefing session.

High on the agenda for discussion was the salvaged Selestian artifacts, which stood to disprove the unfounded accusations and claims made by evangelist Graham James - views subscribed to by a growing number of other prominent religious leaders.

"I think the opportune moment is fast approaching when we can let the world know about the alien treasures," announced Stanwick, after first complimenting the crew for their heroic behavior in the face of adversity.

"How do you propose to break the news?" asked Thompson.

"We've arranged an internationally televised program, before a large live audience, during which we intend to demonstrate the Selestian holographic cube projector," Stanwick answered.

"When is this event scheduled?" Duncan inquired.

"Three days from now," replied the chairman.

In certain respects the timing could hardly have been better. The very day prior to the planned broadcast, a consortium of the world's most prestigious religious authorities publicly agreed with essentials of the evangelist's views. Even the pope could not resist making a statement, urging all members of his flock to: "beware of false prophets from space who would deny the Divinity of Christ/Jesus." Stopping short of openly accepting the "murder" theory advanced by James, he nevertheless saw fit to praise him for his courageous stand in defending the faith.

When the big day finally arrived, it was before a packed Miami auditorium audience estimated to exceed 40,000 inquisitive souls. Amidst unprecedented security precautions, all seven crew members were introduced and given a thunderous ovation. Four giant TV screens displayed video highlights of the expedition, reviving old memories and thoughts of what might have been. High resolution pictures of the "Face" were shown, followed by views of the deep 30 kilometer crater left by the explosion of the Selestian matter/ antimatter reactor. More than a few eyebrows were raised when a number of respected physicists pointed out that the crater was considerably larger than what could have been produced by Earth's most powerful hydrogen bomb!

A second punch against the "hoax" syndrome was delivered when the alien cube projector was introduced. Having earlier previewed hundreds of Selestian images, Stanwick was confident that their planned program would convince even a hardened skeptic. Inserting one of the diminutive cubes into the tiny projector, it was not long before live audience and television viewer alike were quite astonished at the size and incredible clarity of the holographic image which formed before their very eyes. In the span of the next hour some 300 different images were projected, including both interior and exterior views of the "Face," the great alien starships and, finally, literally dozens of scenes of the Selestian's home world.

The science involved in these truly fascinating 3-D images was clearly well beyond current Earth technology. Not only was the image quality positively astounding for such a small projector, but the power source - believed to be a miniature battery of some kind - totally defied explanation by the best scientific minds. There was simply no way that any critic could conjure up an excuse to deny the alien nature of the device.

The holographic projector session was immediately followed by news of a second treasure to be rescued. The magic elixir, which could extend the youthful functions and features of human life by as much as 300%, had been salvaged by the astronauts just prior to the explosion. Moreover, it could be made freely available to all of Earth society. The chief regret was that the scourge of cancer would still be with mankind, as it had been impossible to save the wondrous alien machine in view of the impending blast - a disaster perpetrated by a criminal act of the highest magnitude, and in the very name of religion!

To emphasize this point, Stanwick next produced a number of surprise witnesses who testified that both Manzoni and Alvarez had strong ties to evangelist Graham James. In fact, it was shown that large sums of money had been surreptitiously transferred to bank accounts held jointly with their wives - money which (after much difficulty) had been traced to James' TV ministry. In turn, the funds were revealed to have originated from several extremely wealthy businessmen. Withheld from the public until the most opportune moment, this evidence would now be used to indict James and his associates. Criminal charges had already been prepared, it was announced, and would shortly be filed against those who were responsible for committing such a dastardly act of sabotage and murder.

By way of concluding the historic program, Professor Duncan was asked to speak on behalf of the Mars astronauts. Accepting the opportunity, he made an earnest plea for the inhabitants of all nations to cease their petty squabbling over religious views which, he maintained, *were really the inherited beliefs of others!* Indeed, had most people not been so deeply exposed to such ideas, they would never have thought of them during the span of their entire lifetime. Instead, he urged individuals to think for themselves, and to use logic and the revelations of science in order to formulate their own philosophy of life. The superior wisdom of the Selestians, in his opinion, clearly warranted both serious consideration and emulation. Not only did mankind have much to learn with regard to religion/philosophy, but also with respect to social and economic issues. He ended his brief address by calling for a new United Nations/World Organization - one that would have the power and will to act swiftly and decisively to disarm nations and to remove from authority any obnoxious government which would resort to warfare or deny the basic rights of an individual.

The next three days produced several startling developments. Confronted with proof of his involvement in the Martian atrocity, Graham James and six of his close associates committed suicide rather than face utter humiliation and serious criminal charges. Other religious leaders (including the pope) frantically strived to distance themselves from the zealots, having just recently seen fit to extend nothing but praise. Unfortunately, as is so often the case when the masses let emotions run wild, acts of violence are to be expected. Inflamed by the treachery of their religious leaders, and angered by the loss of a cure for cancer, groups of vigilantes began a campaign of church burning. Within one month literally thousands of churches, mosques and synagogues were put to the torch worldwide in spontaneous acts of vengeance. Quite regrettably, the pendulum had now swung too far in the opposite direction.

At long last it had become evident that a key ingredient for world harmony was an individual's need for freedom of information - especially with regard to the issue of religious indoctrination. In essence, it was finally recognized that it was an injustice to exclude a child from insight into other religions and into other philosophies. The hitherto assumed right of parents to thrust their particular views upon innocent offspring - to the exclusion of alternate concepts - was now exposed as a great mistake and a detriment to society. Not only did it divide a civilization into a number of opposing religious and cultural factions, but this very practice prevented the normal advance and evolution of ideas by nurturing old views and old prejudices long past the point where they should have been discarded.

Nor was global revolution restricted to issues of a religious nature. Change was definitely in the wind on several additional fronts. Although the Selestian's social wisdom had been public knowledge for some time, recent events had motivated a demand for reform - with greater economic equality being high on the list of needed improvements. Inspired by a series of lectures, delivered by Professor Duncan, there was a public outcry for adopting many facets of the economic and social philosophy of the aliens. In short order a host of new political parties sprang up, offering hope of replacing many corrupt and unjust governments. A prime requisite for reform was a strict limitation upon both wealth and income - a reform which, at long last, would allow the principle of democracy to achieve its hitherto unfulfilled potential.

Seven months after the Mars astronauts had returned to Earth, certain significant events occurred in their personal lives. Matt and Erica Duncan became the proud parents of healthy twins, Martin and Marcia. In all the annals of human space flight they were the first set of twins to be conceived beyond the domain of their own planet's gravitational field. At about this same time one of the larger movie studios finalized plans for a rather elaborate 3-D production based on the drama which had just transpired. Entitled "The Face on Mars," it would feature in its cast as many of the original astronauts as possible. Adam Thompson, in particular, looked forward to being reunited with Martin Chadwick, his old colleague from the initial expedition. (Released one year later, the movie proved to be an instant box office hit, far surpassing all expectation.)

Partly as a result of the very favorable publicity, Professor Duncan was subsequently invited to become the chairman of a new and totally restructured World Society, born out of the ashes of an old and inept United Nations. Upon accepting the post, he soon pressed for the establishment of a World Government and a common world language. Perhaps, with much perseverance, it would yet be possible for Earth civilization to mature sufficiently to merit acceptance by the Selestians when they arrived in one of their great starships.

It had taken a severe shock to incense an indifferent and misguided populace, but once aroused the masses generated a force which promised to sweep across cultural and ethnic boundaries. While the "Face" on Mars was no more, it had offered them a legacy rich in moral and philosophical values. It was destined to be acknowledged that mankind's surprise contact, with a superior race of beings, was an occasion of momentous importance - completely eclipsing all previous historical events. Although a wealth of scientific and technological information had been lost through man's greed and folly, in the last analysis the world had been given far more: an enhanced perspective with regard to a host of philosophical issues and cosmic mysteries!